NAME: Elizabeth Ann Jackson. Liz for short, Elizabeth when I'm in trouble.

AGE: Almost a teenager.

HAIR: On a good day, tumbling auburn curls. On a bad day, a brownish-reddish bush.

EYES: Midnight blue, sapphire blue, deep sea blue – take your pick.

STAR SIGN: Taurus the bull. Don't even go there.

LOVES: Pizza. Pizza delivery guy. White Musk perfume. Best friend Bumble. Kittens. Painting. Eminem.

HATES: Horrible neighbour. Mam being gone. Lemon meringue pies. Dad's lumpy porridge. Mam being gone. Not having a mobile phone. Mam being gone.

Born in Kerry, Roisin Meaney is a primary school teacher living in Limerick. She is a published author of adult fiction: *The Daisy Picker* (Tivoli, 2004) and *Putting Out the Stars* (Tivoli, 2005). *Don't Even Think About It* is her first novel for children.

don't Even Think About it

ROISIN MEANEY

THE O'BRIEN PRESS
DUBLIN

First published 2006 by The O'Brien Press Ltd.
12 Terenure Road East, Dublin 6, Ireland.
Tel: +353 1 4923333; Fax: +353 1 4922777
E-mail: books@obrien.ie
Website: www.obrien.ie

ISBN-10: 0-86278-984-2
ISBN-13: 978-0-86278-984-8

British Library Cataloguing-in-Publication Data
Meaney, Roisin
Don't even think about it
1. Diary fiction 2. Children's stories
I. Title
823.9'2[J]

1 2 3 4 5 6
06 07 08 09 10

The O'Brien Press receives assistance from

Editing, typesetting and design: The O'Brien Press Ltd
Printed and bound in the UK by CPI Group

To Tadhg, Fiachra, Eoghan and Bríd, with love.

Acknowledgements

Many thanks to my two coaches, Bríd Moriarty and Eimear Duff, who clued me in on all sorts of teenage girl stuff, to the children of The Limerick School Project for giving me plenty of raw material to work with, to my editor Susan Houlden and her very helpful daughter Hannah, who read and critiqued my earlier drafts, and to all at O'Brien Press.

Ten to ten, Saturday, March, haven't a clue what date.
Dad is such a grouch these days, giving out about every
little thing. Here are a few of his favourite moans:

> DON'T leave your shoes lying around.
> How many times have I told you NOT to bang
> the door?
> DON'T talk back to me.
> WATCH your language.
> Turn DOWN that music.

Sometimes I think I can't do anything right. I've just
been sent to my room now, over something really silly.
OK, I probably shouldn't have thrown the bowl at him,
but talk about over-reacting.

Funny, I never noticed that crack in the ceiling. Serve
Dad right if the whole thing fell on top of me. He
probably wouldn't even notice I was missing, until the

school phoned on Monday to see why I wasn't coming in. Then he'd come upstairs and find me squashed flat under bits of the ceiling, and he'd be totally devastated. Serve him right, the big fat grouch.

Twenty-five past ten

OK, I've just painted my nails Orange Blossom. We're not allowed nail varnish in school so I'll have to clean it off tomorrow night. Talk about a stupid rule – as if the colour of your nails matters in school. What has that got to do with anything? You don't think with your nails, do you? You don't write with your nails – well, you do, kind of, but you know what I mean.

My nails are all bitten. I never used to bite them till a few months ago, and then one day I just started. Now I can't stop. I'm a nail-biting addict.

Actually, that orange nail varnish is kind of gross – I may as well take it off now. Give me something to do.

Five to eleven

Right, I have been up in this room for over an hour, and boy, does it feel like forever. I can't read because I've finished my library books. And I can't even play Slim Shady at top volume to annoy Dad – naturally, he can't bear Eminem – because I spilt Coke on my CD player last week, and now it just makes a funny noise, kind of a clickety buzz, when you switch it on. I tried to suck out the Coke with a straw but it didn't help. I might try blow-drying it.

I could do some painting, I suppose, but I'm too cranky for watercolours right now. And anyway, the floor is covered with my clothes – I might get paint on them.

I suppose I could tidy my room. Ha ha.

Boy, I am SO bored. Bugger, bugger, bugger.

Dad hates me saying Bugger. He should hear some of the stuff I say when he's not around.

You're probably wondering why I threw a bowl at him. Actually it was really the porridge I was throwing – it just happened to be in the bowl at the time.

My Dad makes the worst porridge ever – I mean the WORST. D'you know what porridge lumps remind me of? (WARNING: Don't read this if you've got a weak stomach or something – just skip on a bit.)

down to here

Porridge lumps remind me of warts. Big, warm, lumpy warts that slither down your throat and make you feel like puking.

And Dad's porridge is *always* lumpy – and too thick as well, so you can't cool it down with milk. A few days ago I burnt my tongue trying to eat the stuff, and I had to stick it into a glass of iced water. My tongue I mean, not the porridge. That might sound funny to you, but believe me, I wasn't laughing at the time. (Neither was Dad – he knows what my temper's like.)

So anyway, this morning I just couldn't face the thought of forcing those horrible lumps down again, so I told Dad I didn't feel like any porridge. He put a scowl on, because he's always extra grumpy in the morning, and said, 'Well, there's nothing else.' So I said I'd have nothing then.

And for once I wasn't trying to be cheeky. I really didn't care whether I had breakfast or not. I knew I could get a burger in town later with Bumble, but of course Dad got all narky and slopped a huge dollop of porridge into a bowl and thumped it down in front of me and said, 'I've already made it, so you'll eat it.'

Now, I don't know about you, but when someone tells me I have to do something that I really don't want to do, it makes me pretty mad. So that made two mad people in one fairly small kitchen, which was what Granny Daly would call *A RECIPE FOR DISASTER*.

I sat there for a few minutes, feeling kind of prickly and looking at the grey, lumpy mess in front of me, and then – I don't know, I didn't plan it, but something just made me pick up the bowl and throw it at him.

Now, I know it wasn't the most sensible thing to do, but I really can't understand why he got so cross. The bowl didn't even hit him – it sailed right past him and hit the wall.

(NOTE TO SELF: Practise my aim.)

It didn't break either, which I thought was pretty amazing. I mean, what are the chances? I must try it again sometime when Dad's not around. I'll do best of three – we've loads of bowls, and a lot of them are cracked already.

Anyway, Dad started roaring at me to go to my room, which was actually kind of a relief, since I thought he might make me clean it up, and that would have been pretty gross. Imagine trying to mop up those warty lumps – yeuk. So I cleared out of there fast, before he could change his mind, and here I am for the rest of the day, as usual.

You'd think he could come up with a few different punishments now and again. He could make me eat the jelly with the furry stuff on top that's been sitting in the fridge for the past week, or clean the toilet with my toothbrush or something. He has NO imagination.

Sometimes I think he looks for something to fight with me about, which is so unfair.

I mean, it's not my fault that Mam left. It was HIM she couldn't live with, not me.

Twenty-five past eleven

When Mam told me she was going, it felt like the end of the world – or the end of *my* world, anyway.

I couldn't understand how she could just leave me like that. Just fill up her two matching red suitcases, and her starry make-up case with the furry pompom on the zip that I gave her last Christmas, and just walk away from me. Well, not walk – she drove away in her Clio – but you know what I mean.

Of course I knew that things were bad between her and Dad. Here's the kind of stuff that was going on:

1. They didn't talk to each other, except when they had to.
2. They never went out together, just the two of them.
3. They didn't look at each other when they spoke.
4. They didn't use each other's names.
5. Their voices were awful, all polite and cold.
6. They stopped laughing.

I think it was the no-laughing bit I noticed first. I think it was then I started to bite my nails.

So anyway, Mam came up to my room the day after

11

Christmas, where I was trying out my new watercolour paints (and making a right mess) and she sat on my bed and said in a quiet voice that she had something to tell me.

I looked at her face and I knew, I just knew what she was going to say. I wanted to put my hand over her mouth and stop the words coming out. I wanted to tell her that it was OK, that I didn't mind about her and Dad not liking each other any more, or about the awful feeling in the air sometimes, when the three of us were in the same room together. I wanted to tell her that I could live with it, that we could all live with it.

Together, in this house, where we all belonged.

But I didn't do or say anything. I just looked at her with the most awful feeling inside me, as if every bit of me was sinking slowly down to my toes, trying to get away.

And then Mam started talking, and as soon as she did, I panicked and butted in, and tried to show her my picture, shoved it right in front of her and said, 'Look, Mam, look what I did. See the brown bit there, in front of the tree? It's going to be a horse, but I'm not sure if I made him too big. What do you think, Mam? Should I make him smaller?'

And she waited until I stopped talking, and then she made me sit on the bed beside her, and she put her arm around my shoulder and she said that she was leaving, that she had to leave. And that she knew how hard it was going to be for me, and how sorry she was that she had to do it, and how it wasn't my fault, how I had done nothing wrong. And lots more horrible stuff like that.

And I tried not to listen, but I had to, because her arm was still around my shoulder and I couldn't move. And then these giant tears came out of nowhere and just spilled out of my eyes, and I let them. And some of them splashed onto the painting that was still sitting in my lap, and made it even wetter than it had been before. I could hear the little plops, and see the splodges they made on the paper. That horse was history.

When Mam finished talking, when she finished promising that she'd phone me every single day, I wiped the tears away with my sleeve and I told her that she wouldn't have to phone me, because I was coming with her. I could pack right away; it would only take a few minutes.

And she squeezed my shoulder and said no, she couldn't do that to me, she couldn't take me away from my home, and from Dad. Not now anyway, not when she hadn't a clue where she was going, or what kind of place she was going to be living in.

Didn't she know I couldn't care less where we lived, that we could sleep in doorways for all I cared, with smelly old blankets and rats running over us, as long as we were together? I didn't say that though, because I just knew by her face that it wouldn't do any good. When grown-ups make up their minds to do something, there's no way us kids are going to change them. Sad, but true.

Then she told me she was going to leave with Granny Daly (her mother) after lunch. Granny had been staying with us over Christmas like she always did, and Mam wasn't due to drive her home for another three days.

So that meant she couldn't even bear to stay three more days with us. Mam, I mean, not Granny Daly.

I think that's when I stopped feeling sad and began to feel angry. I didn't say any more, just listened to her telling me again how much she'd miss me, and how she'd call me often, and I heard myself saying, 'Yeah, right' in my head. YEAH RIGHT   YEAH RIGHT   YEAH RIGHT

Of course, when she left, when she and Granny Daly drove off in the Clio, all I felt was lonely. I stood by myself and watched the car disappearing around the end of the road – Dad hadn't come out to see them off, which wasn't surprising – and I could still feel Mam's arms from the last hug she gave me.

I didn't hug her back. I wish I had now.

She called that evening from Granny Daly's, just after Dad and I had eaten the turkey sandwiches that neither of us wanted. Here's what I remember of that call:

Her: Hi darling.
Me: Hi. (My eyes filled with tears as soon as I heard her voice.)
Her: Are you OK?
Me: Yeah, never better. (I had to bite my cheek hard to stop my voice from wobbling.)
Her: (Big sigh) I'm so sorry, love. I know this is hard for you.
Me: Yeah, right.
Her: I understand if you're mad at me. You have every right to be.
Me: Yeah. (Trying my best to sound bored.)

Anyway, you get the idea. Mam did most of the talking and I did most of the pretending not to care. She told me she'd be staying with Granny for a little while till she decided what she was going to do, and that she missed me a lot, and that she wished things could be different. I leant against the wall and twirled the phone cord and just kept saying 'Yeah.'

After a while it got too hard to keep talking to her, so I told her there was a film coming on telly, and she sighed again and told me she'd call the next day.

As soon as I hung up, I got the strictly-for-special-occasions tub of Ben & Jerry's out of the freezer and attacked it with the biggest spoon I could find. Dad didn't say anything when he saw me, but the next time I looked in the freezer there were two new tubs there.

For the rest of the Christmas holidays, I felt horribly lonely. Not mad, just lonely. Except when I was in bed, lying in the dark, and then I felt scared too. What if something happened to Dad, and I was left all alone in the house? I'm only twelve, for God's sake.

I told Bumble that Mam was gone. Bumble is my best friend, and he and Mam always got on really well. He was shocked when I told him, and he didn't say anything for a while. Then he said, 'She must have been really unhappy if she could leave you.'

And you know what? I hadn't thought of it that way at all. I never really thought about how sad *she* must have felt – I was too busy feeling bad for myself. And it didn't make me feel much better really, but it helped a bit, in a weird kind of way, to remember that I wasn't the only one hurting.

I love Bumble. He's the greatest best friend anyone could have.

Mam phoned me every day, usually around teatime. I don't know how I felt about those calls. Part of me wanted to leave the house when I knew she was going to ring, just to show her that we could manage fine without her, but I never did. I sat in my room and tried to paint, and the minute the phone rang I flew down the stairs and stood beside it until it had rung six times, and then I picked it up and said 'Hello?' really casually, as if I couldn't care less who it was.

Dad never answered the phone around teatime. The one time I wasn't there, when I was having tea at Bumble's, he just let it ring.

We didn't talk about much on the phone, me and Mam. I always asked her how Granny Daly was, and she always said that she missed me, and the rest of the time we just filled with silly stuff like the weather, and what we each had for dinner. She never asked about Dad.

It's got a little bit easier since those first few calls, but I still have mixed feelings about talking to her on the phone. I feel that somehow I'm being mean to Dad, although I know that's silly.

Dad and I muddled through the days without Mam. He never mentioned her, and neither did I. We went shopping together on the Saturday after she left, and he let me get any kind of food I wanted.

On Tuesday we ran out of toilet rolls, and on Thursday I had to wash my hair in washing-up liquid, and by the end of the week I never wanted to see another pop tart. We got better at the shopping after that. I'd make a list before we went, and we'd do our best to stick to it.

And then, just when I was beginning to cope with Mam not being there, two really horrible things happened:

1. Dad decided he'd start making porridge for breakfast, like Mam used to.
2. Mam told me she was moving back to San Francisco, where she'd been working before she married Dad.

Here's how *that* phone call went:

Her: Guess what – I've been offered my old job back, in San Francisco. (She wrote for some dorky magazine out there, about a million years ago.)

Mc: (Silence. I was too shocked to say anything.)

Her: Are you still there?

Me: I can't believe it. You're moving to America?

Her: Listen love, I'll still phone you every day, OK? I promise. It'll be just the same as now, honest.

Me: Yeah, RIGHT. It'll be exactly the same when you're thousands of miles away.

Her: OK, I know it's a lot to take in, but please love, try to –

And that was all I heard, because I had just hung up. Can you believe it? She was planning to go and live in America, leaving her only child behind her, and she had the cheek to sound excited about it. In case you don't know exactly where San Francisco is, it's right over on the far side of America, about a zillion miles away.

Of course she phoned back, right away. I stood beside the phone feeling mad as hell. I let it ring six times, and then I picked it up and put it down again without even listening. And then I took it off the hook and went straight to the freezer.

After half an hour I put it back, and she called ten minutes later, and I just about managed not to tell her what I thought of her brilliant plan.

I told Dad she was moving, because I thought he should know. It was the first time I mentioned Mam to him since she'd left. Dad just nodded and went on eating Marjorie Maloney's tuna casserole.

I'll get to Marjorie Maloney later.

And now Mam has been in San Francisco for about two months, and she still rings me every day, and her voice still sounds as near as when she was ringing from Granny Daly's house.

But she's not in Granny Daly's house – she's ten hours on a plane away from here, and I have no idea when I'll see her again.

OK, I have to stop for a while now.

A quarter to one

The day after Mam's bombshell about San Francisco, the Christmas holidays ended and I went back to school (I'm in sixth, by the way). I couldn't tell anyone what had happened, I just couldn't – except for Bumble, of course. So I told the rest of the class that

Mam had gone off to be a nun in one of those convents where they aren't allowed to talk to anyone from the outside world, which was why Dad and I couldn't visit her.

Naturally, Catherine Eggleston had something to say. She said, 'Married women aren't allowed to become nuns'. So I said, quick as a flash, 'Oh, didn't you know? The Pope changed that law two years ago, when there was a shortage of nuns.'

Well, that shut Catherine Eggleston up, and everyone else too, because of course nobody had a clue whether that was true or not. They all looked a bit sorry for me, and Chloe Nelligan offered me her Penguin bar at break, which I refused – I could see that really impressed them all. I didn't tell them that I hate Penguins, and that I'd been hoping that Tessa Ryan would offer me her mini Bounty bar. I love Bounty bars.

Of course, I'm still hoping like mad that Mam will realise that she made a terrible mistake and come home. I try to pray for it to happen, but I'm not very good at praying. Whenever I try, I can't stop other things jumping into my head, like whether I remembered to bring home my maths copy, or how many days left to my birthday, things like that.

But I really, really hope she comes back.

I wonder if Dad misses her as much as I do. No, of course he doesn't.

Ten past one

God, I am SO starving right now. I could eat a slice of stale bread that fell on a carpet, buttery side up. I wouldn't even pick off the bits of hair and stuff – I'd just cram it all into my mouth.

This must be what it's like to go on hunger strike. Oh God, I smell food. It can't be coming from downstairs – he never cooks anything that smells this good. Must be the Wallace's lunch next door. Smells like melting cheese – oh God, I think I'm going to start dribbling.

My stomach is making incredibly loud gurgly noises. When I get out of here I'm going to look up the Childline number in the phone book and report my father for starving his only child.

OK, he just knocked on the door after I wrote that last bit and told me he was leaving my lunch on a tray outside. I didn't bother answering him. He must be dreaming if he thinks I'm going anywhere near it.

I am SO starving though. Bugger, bugger, bugger.

Twenty-five past one

Listen, the only reason I ate it was because I thought there was a really strong chance that I was going to collapse with starvation, which would mean never seeing Mam again. Imagine how she'd feel if she came back from America and found me dead.

I did it for her, not for me.

It turned out to be a pizza, one of those frozen ones. Simple enough for even my dad to cook. Boy, was it good. I nearly licked the plate.

OK, I did lick the plate.

Not that it lets him off though. No way. He's still a grouch who cooks warty porridge and then tortures people by starving them.

Now I'm really thirsty. Maybe I'll take the can of Coke I was planning to leave outside the door. Look, he probably wouldn't even notice if I left it there – and anyway, he doesn't drink Coke, so if I don't have it, I'll be just letting it go to waste, which I'm pretty sure is a sin.

Half past one

OK, Dad just knocked again and said I can come out if I apologise. I was tempted to tell him to get stuffed, but then I remembered that I wanted to change my library books, so I said I'd think about it. He gave a kind of a snort and went away. I'll make him wait ten minutes before I go downstairs.

TROUBLE

Five o'clock, Thursday, somewhere near the beginning of April.
Today I got into trouble at school. Again. Another visit
to Smelly Nelly's office – and a note for Dad, which I'll
get to later.

Smelly Nelly is our principal. Her real name is Mrs
Nelligan, and her breath always stinks of garlic, so you
can see where the name comes from. She has a daughter
called Chloe in my class – remember the one with the
Penguin bar? – and she's a garlic freak too. Nobody can
stand being around her, especially on Mondays. They
must spend the weekend eating garlic. No danger of
vampires in Nelligans' house, that's for sure.

Anyway, all I did today was pass on a note. I didn't
even write the stupid thing. It just landed on my desk,
and when I looked around to see who'd thrown it,
Catherine Eggleston put a horrible smarmy smile on
her face and pointed to Terry McNamara, who was on
the other side of me.

Catherine Eggleston doesn't like me, and boy, is the feeling mutual. But I didn't want to leave the note on my desk, and Terry sometimes lets me look into his copy at maths time, so I decided to pass it on.

Of course I had to read it first – well, I was doing them a favour, they owed me – so I held it under the desk and opened it, feeling Catherine's eyes boring into me from behind.

Boy, was it a big disappointment. All it said was:

> 'Don't believe all you hear. Trudy has a vivid imagenation.'

I had no idea what it meant – except that Catherine Eggleston couldn't spell imagination – so I folded it again and reached across to Terry, and I was just handing it to him when Santa turned around from the blackboard and caught me.

Santa is our teacher. His name is Mr Santorio, even though he's Irish, but his grandfather or someone came from Italy. Santa doesn't look in the least like an Italian man, who as far as I know are all dark and good looking, and probably tall.

Santa is the complete opposite – small with wavy red hair that grows in his ears as well as on his head, and his eyes are blue, not chocolate brown, and they're a bit crossed as well, so you're never quite sure if he's looking at you.

But the fact that he roared out 'Elizabeth Jackson' gave me a pretty good idea who he was looking at. That's my name, Elizabeth Jackson, although most people call me Liz. Anyway, Santa made me bring up the note, and my heart sank, because I knew I was off to Smelly's office again.

The last time I was there was only about ten days before, after the dead beetle in Trudy Higgins's cheese sandwich. She nearly ate it too, before she spotted its legs, or something, sticking out. You should have heard the scream she let out – I'd say half the school heard it. And then of course her best buddy, Catherine Eggleston, came running over and screeched her head off too. Talk about drama queens.

I still don't know how they guessed it was me, though. I mean, I hadn't made a big deal out of Trudy laughing at my banana sandwich the day before, just told her to belt up. How was I supposed to know that bananas go black in sandwiches? Mam had always made my lunch – I was just learning what you could and couldn't put into a sandwich:

Yes	No
Cheese	Tomatoes
Peanut Butter	Bananas
Ham	Curry sauce
Nutella	Ben & Jerry's
Crisps	Baked beans

And of course Santa believed Trudy when she pointed a shaking finger in my direction and whimpered, 'She did it, I know she did,' and off I went to the office.

So today Smelly gave her usual 'I'm-very-disappointed-in-you' talk, and I did my best to look sorry – I knew there was no point in telling her I hadn't written the note – and then I was sent back to apologise to Santa.

And just before home time, when I thought it was all over, Smelly called into the class and handed me an envelope to bring home to Dad, and told me to get him to sign the note inside and to bring it back to her tomorrow. Bugger.

I've just opened it – well, Smelly never said I couldn't – and here's what it says:

Dear Mr Jackson,

I'm sorry to have to bother you, particularly in the light of your recent domestic problems –

Domestic problems? What's she on about?

– but I have to tell you that Elizabeth has been increasingly disruptive in class since Christmas. She has been sent to my office six times during that period, for various reasons –

Six times? No way – it was definitely no more than three. Definitely.

– and for her own sake, and the sake of her classmates, something needs to be done, particularly in the light of her imminent transition to secondary school.

Imminent transition? I have no idea what that means. Why can't people use normal words?

I am sure a word from you will be effective, and will hopefully sort things out.

Many thanks,

G Nelligan, principal

G. Probably stands for Godzilla.

OK, I've thought about it, and I hate to admit it, but Smelly is right, I *have* been to her office six times since Christmas:

1.   The dead beetle.
2.   The note today, which I didn't even write.
3.   The encyclopaedia I dropped on the floor, which of course was an accident. (It sure gave Santa a fright though.)
4.   That drawing I did after our 'how babies are made' class – just a cartoon, not rude at all really.
5.   Copying the way Santa stood on tiptoe to reach the top of the blackboard – not exactly a major crime.
6.   The poem I wrote about Santa, which I thought was very creative.

Yes, that does make six times. I should have known Smelly would have her facts right. Bugger.

And I suppose 'domestic problems' is about Mam leaving – not that that has anything to do with my ending up in Smelly's office. Oh well, I'd better face the music. I still have to show the note to Dad, and I heard him coming in from work a few minutes ago. Wish me luck.

Could have been worse. I'm just forbidden to watch TV for the rest of the week. He's probably forgotten that this is Thursday. Saturday is the end of the week, right? So that's just three nights. No problem.

And by the way, in case you're wondering, I'm a latchkey kid since Mam left, which means I have to let myself into an empty house every day after school, and wait about two hours till Dad gets home. I have a good mind to report him to Childline for *that*.

Although I must say it's kind of cool to have the house to myself. Mam never used to let me watch telly in the afternoons.

Nearly time for her phone call. Guess what I'm not going to tell her.

Five past five, Friday, 23rd April.
Today is my thirteenth birthday. I am the first official teenager in the class. What's more, I'm a teenager from a broken home.

As Granny Daly would say, *A RECIPE FOR DISASTER.*

Granny Daly knows a lot of recipes for disaster.

I got a Dunnes jumper and a twenty euro book token from Dad, and luckily he left the tag on the jumper, so I can bring it back after school tomorrow and swap it for something that doesn't look like it was bought by someone who has NO IDEA what thirteen-year-old girls are wearing these days.

And I might be able to trade the book token for cash with Mary Sullivan, who always has her nose stuck in a book.

Dad's cooking is as bad as ever. Last night we had potatoes with hard bits in the middle of them, and burnt fish fingers. Even I can do fish fingers without burning them. Tonight we're going out for a Chinese, thank goodness.

I wonder if Dad would let me have some wine, now that I'm thirteen. It can't taste any worse than the sherry I swiped from the sitting-room cabinet last month. God, that was BAD. It must have been past its sell-by-date, or something.

I got half a bottle of White Musk perfume from Bumble – I told him what I wanted and gave him half the money, because it's a bit dear. Bumble is great at lots of things, but he's useless at buying presents.

Last year he gave me a yellow Eminem baseball hat, which just goes to show. My best friend since we were four years old, and he gets me a hat in my least favourite colour. I HATE yellow anything – yellow buildings, yellow flowers, yellow cars. The only yellow things I like are the sun and bananas. Oh, and corn on the cob. And the yellow bit of a boiled egg, as long as it's soft and runny.

Anyway, I had to wear the Eminem hat a few times so Bumble's feelings wouldn't be hurt – mostly around the house – and then I pretended that I'd left it in the garden and the Wallaces' cat next door had peed in it, and I couldn't bring myself to wear it again after that. He believed me, of course. Bumble's nice like that.

So this year I was taking no chances. I love White Musk. It makes me feel sexy and dangerous. Pity it makes Bumble want to throw up, but you can't have everything.

Bumble's name isn't really Bumble, of course – it's

Ben. When he was small someone shortened it to B, and then later someone else changed it to Bumble Bee, and now it's just Bumble. He doesn't mind; he's very easy-going.

Granny Daly sent me a new hairbrush, which I thought was quite a good present for someone with hair that you can actually brush, unlike mine which is too curly for anything except one of those big wooden combs.

By the way, in case you're wondering, I have reddish brown hair, just longer than my shoulders, and dark blue eyes and zillions of freckles, and a dimple in my chin that I absolutely HATE. I'm 156 centimetres tall and I wear size 38 shoes and my teeth are almost perfectly straight, with a tiny gap between the front two that's great for spitting through, and I have no boobs yet, and I'm Eminem's biggest fan, and I can't bear Britney, and I think Colin Farrell is the sexiest man on the planet.

My favourite food is pizza – but I eat most things – and one of my biggest fears is getting stuck in a lift halfway up a skyscraper. And you've already figured that I'm an only child, and my parents are split up. So now you know.

I'll offer the hairbrush to Bumble's brother's girlfriend, whose hair sure could use a bit of brushing. She might trade me one of her bangles for it – they're really cool, and she has loads.

I got a fiver from Marjorie Maloney, a neighbour across the road, but that's only because she has her eye on Dad since Mam left. She pestered us the first month, knocking on the back door at least twice a week with casseroles, and lemon meringue pie, which is one of the few foods I hate, and asking Dad if he'd have a look at her iron – probably broke it on purpose – and offering to take me shopping for clothes and stuff. As if.

A few times we pretended to be out, but she just came back half an hour later, so we gave that up. The Wallaces' cat next door got a lot of leftover casseroles for a few weeks. He loved the tuna ones, but he turned up his nose at the chicken, probably because Marjorie Maloney put lots of herbs and stuff in, trying to impress Dad.

Honestly, the way she plays with her hair and giggles when Dad says anything makes me want to throw up in her face. As if he'd look at Marjorie Maloney in a million years, with her tight dresses that stretch across her behind and show the line of her knickers, which everyone knows is a fashion disaster.

Her hair is dyed too – it has to be. No way is anyone's hair that black. And the perfume she wears is strong enough to knock out an elephant, and nowhere near as sexy as White Musk.

Oh, and I got a parcel.

It arrived a day early, which I suppose is OK seeing as how it came all the way from San Francisco. There was nobody here when the Post Office van delivered it, so Mrs Wallace from next door took it in, and her son Damien came around with it when I got home from school.

I haven't opened it yet. It's sitting on my desk in front of me, and it's about twice the size of a shoebox and fairly heavy. It cost $14.25 to post, and on the back Mam has written her name and address. She lives in a part of San Francisco called The Mission, which she says is a good place to live as she can walk to the downtown area where she works.

It's the first time she's ever written to me.

It's the first time she hasn't been here for my birthday.

I'm wondering why it's so hard to open the box.

She's sharing an apartment with a couple called Enda and George. She still tells me she misses me every time she phones, and she hopes I'm eating properly. I don't mention the pizzas, or the Coke. She asks me about school, and Bumble, and how my painting is coming along, and she never, ever mentions Dad.

It's easier now, talking to her on the phone, even if she's still the one doing most of the talking. Dad always gets out of the way, which is nice of him. It still makes me sad that she's so far away, of course, and I hate the time right after I hang up. I usually make straight for the freezer. I'm getting through a tub and a half of Ben & Jerry's every week.

And now it's getting near time to go out to dinner, and I heard Dad coming home a while ago, and I'm sitting in my room looking at the box on my desk, trying to pluck up the courage to open it.

You'd swear there was a bomb inside it.

I couldn't think about anything else all day. For once, Santa didn't have to give out to me for anything. And at break, Bumble asked me why I was so quiet. He'd just given me the White Musk, and I'd dabbed it on my wrists, and I could see him breathing through his mouth to stop himself from throwing up.

And for once, I couldn't tell him. Even though he's the only person I told about Mam walking out on us, I just couldn't mention the box. I muttered something about missing Mam, and he nodded, and spent the rest of the break trying to cheer me up with his awful jokes, and I smiled to keep him happy.

And now I can't put it off any more, so here goes.

Half past seven

Dad was brilliant. He didn't say anything, which was exactly what I wanted, just put down the newspaper and held out his arms when I came into the sitting room, and held me until I was totally out of tears. And that took a while, believe me.

When I finally dried up, Dad said, 'What about doing the Chinese meal tomorrow night instead?' and when I nodded, he went into the kitchen and came back with a tub of Ben & Jerry's New York Super Fudge Chunk that was only half-empty, and two spoons. And while we ate it, he told me that he knew how hard it was for me without Mam being here, and that he thought I was coping brilliantly, and that he was really proud of me.

It was the first time he talked to me as if I was a grown-up, which was what I'd been waiting for forever.

And guess what? All I wanted was to be five years old again, so I didn't have to face all this horrible grown-up stuff.

I asked him why Mam had left, why they couldn't have sorted it out, whatever it was, and he shook his head and said that some things just couldn't be sorted out.

And then, without thinking, I said, 'Well then, why couldn't she have taken me with her?' And straight away I was sorry I asked that, because Dad's face kind of crumpled a bit, and I knew I'd hurt him. But he thought about it for a bit, and then he said, 'Maybe because she didn't want me to be left with nobody.' And I thought how much I would have missed him, if Mam *had* taken me with her.

I was really afraid then that he'd ask me if I'd rather have gone and lived with Mam, which would have been impossible to answer. I mean, I think I probably *would* rather be with her, if I absolutely had to choose – maybe because Mam and I are both females – but whoever I lived with, I'd end up missing the other one terribly.

He didn't ask me, though. Maybe he already knew the answer. Maybe parents know more than we think.

The phone rang when we were almost finished the ice cream, and I put down my spoon and walked out to the hall. I knew if I didn't answer it she'd just call back later.

It was awful. As soon as I heard her voice, I wanted to cry again. I had to pinch my arm hard all the way through, while I was trying to sound happy, and thank her for the presents, and tell her the other presents I'd got.

In the end, I said dinner was ready and I had to go. I suppose she knew something was up, but she said nothing. What was there to say?

I took a few deep breaths and went into the kitchen, where I found Dad scrambling some eggs, which sounds strange right after a load of ice cream, but I ate every bit. I suppose it was just dinner the wrong way around. And soon after that I came upstairs again.

My face is hot, and my cheeks feel tight from all the salty water they've had to put up with, and my nose is sore from blowing it so much, but in some kind of a funny way, I feel lighter. I had no idea tears could weigh anything at all. Dad's jumper must be pretty heavy right now, with all the ones I left in it earlier.

Things in the box:

1.   A birthday card with a letter folded up inside
2.   A box of chocolates called See's Candies
3.   A blue t-shirt with a giant ice cream cone on it
4.   A pair of green and blue check pyjama bottoms
5.   A set of three lipsticks
6.   A silver neck chain with a heart on it.

There's a verse on the inside of the card. It reads:

Some say thirteen's unlucky,
But that is SO untrue –
And if you don't believe me,
Just take a look at you!

And here's the letter that fell out of the card:

Darling Liz,

Imagine — you're a teenager! I can't believe my baby is so grown up. I hope you have a wonderful day, and I'm really sorry that I'm not there with you to help you enjoy it.

I know I keep telling you, but I'm going to say it again: I love and miss you very much, and I hate that we can't be together. You'll always be the most important person in the world for me, remember that - it makes no difference how far apart we are.

I hope you like the few little things I'm sending — See's Candies are made in San Francisco, and I think they're yummy! The t-shirt can be worn with the pyjama bottoms, or just on its own as a top in the summer. The necklace is to remind you of how much I love you, and the lipsticks are to have some fun with! (But try to stay away from the boys for another while!)

Happy Birthday darling, thinking of you as always,

Mam xxx

The card has a picture of a girl with long straight brown hair, wearing a pink t-shirt and blue jeans and platform shoes, and balancing a load of shopping in one hand. She's holding a leash in her other hand, and there's a little dog at the end of it with a pink bow in his hair.

I think I'll go to bed now.

RUTH!!!!!!
WALLACE

A quarter past seven, May, a Saturday around the middle. I haven't told you about Ruth Wallace yet, have I? Although I think I've mentioned the Wallaces a few times. They live next door to us, and Ruth is twelve, just a few months younger than me, and she's got brown hair and glasses and a grey cat, and an older brother called Damien. Oh, and she's in a wheelchair.

She doesn't go to my school, so I hardly ever meet her during the week. A white van collects her every morning at ten past eight – I hear it from my bedroom when I'm getting up – and drops her back every afternoon around four.

You can see other kids in the van. One boy waves at everyone the way very little children wave, just flapping his fingers, even though he's about my age. He smiles all the time too. Another girl is hunched over in her wheelchair and never looks up. All you can see is the back of her neck.

Ruth's dad takes his daughter out to the van every morning and waits while they lower the ramp at the back. Then he wheels her on and kisses her goodbye, and he stands, waving, while the van drives off. In the afternoon, her mam comes out, when the van driver sounds the horn, and she wheels Ruth back inside.

And if I could choose a person to live beside, anyone at all in the whole world, Ruth Wallace would be my very last choice.

Now let me explain, because I know how horrible that sounds. You're probably wondering how I can be so mean to my poor disabled neighbour. Well, let me tell you about Ruth Wallace, and then you can decide who the mean one really is.

She lies in wait for me every Saturday in her wheelchair. She sits just inside her gate until she sees me, and then she wheels herself out onto the path and says whatever nasty thing she's been thinking up for me – that I stink, or that my top is horrible, or that I need to use spot cream.

Sometimes she tries to trip me up with her wheels, which is a bit pathetic, because I can easily hop out on the road and dodge around her.

Listen, I'm not making this up. I wish I was, but I'm not. Ruth Wallace is a nasty, cruel person, and I'm the only one who knows it, because, for some reason, she's as nice as apple pie to everyone else. She smiles and looks fragile and says 'Hello' in an innocent little girly voice that makes me want to puke, and they all call her poor Ruth and pat her hand and tell her she's a great girl, and all the time I know what she's like, but I can't tell anyone, because, of course, they wouldn't believe me.

'Ruth, nasty?' they'd say in surprise. 'Why, Liz Jackson, how can you say such a thing? Ruth is so sweet and fragile, and extremely friendly too,' or something like that. That's what they all think, you see.

Ruth wasn't always disabled. Apparently, she got some disease like meningitis when she was only two or three, and she almost died, and since then she hasn't been able to walk. Which is all very sad, of course, but I still don't see why she should be so mean to me. I mean, I didn't make her sick. I didn't take away her legs. Not that her legs are gone – they're still there – but you know what I mean.

I've told Bumble what she's like, because I knew he'd believe me. He thinks Ruth is probably jealous of me being able to walk, and that's what makes her so nasty. When I pointed out that everyone else can walk too, and she's nice to *them*, Bumble said, 'Well, she probably picked you to be mean to because you're handy, living right next door.'

Sometimes I wish Bumble didn't always have an answer for everything.

Ruth's brother Damien is nice, not a bit like her. He's almost sixteen, so I don't hang around with him or anything, but he always smiles and says hello. I wonder what he'd say if he knew what kind of a sister he has.

Today Ruth was waiting for me, as usual, when I came home from town. I could see a bit of her hat poking up from behind the hedge – she always wears a hat, every single day – and my heart sank. I walked quicker, but of course out she came.

She said 'Hello Liz' in a really sickly sweet voice. I didn't look at her, just kept going. And as I passed her, she belted me on the back of the legs with a stick she'd been hiding down the side of her wheelchair. That's what I mean by nasty. For no reason, she just lashed out. It really stung too – I had a red stripe on my legs for about an hour afterwards. But as usual, I said nothing.

Poor Ruth, my foot. She wasn't abandoned by her mother, was she? I bet that's worse than being in a wheelchair. Well, maybe not worse, but definitely as bad, in a different way. At least she has her two parents around.

And she has a brother too, which is more than I have. That was another thing I was sorry about when Mam left, that I hadn't any brothers or sisters, just Dad.

Anyway, that's the story of my nasty neighbour. The Wallaces' cat is nice, all lovely soft grey fur. It's a he – I checked after we had a lesson on cats – and I call him Misty, but that's not his real name. Of course I can't ask Ruth what it is, and I've never heard anyone calling him anything. Mrs Wallace just says 'puss, puss' when she's calling him.

I suppose I just have to put up with the nastiness from Ruth. It can't be much fun being in a wheelchair, even though it means never having to mow the lawn, or take out the bins. But it must be hard to see everyone else running around having fun; it must make her feel really sad. And maybe Bumble's right, maybe she needs someone like me to lash out at sometimes.

I just wish she'd picked someone else, that's all.

Hello again,

Five o'clock, Friday, near the end of May.
We got a new computer yesterday. Well, not brand new
– one they were throwing out from Dad's work – but it's
still in fairly good condition. I told Dad it'd be a big help
to me for doing my homework, and he kind of snorted
and said since when did I become so studious, and I
ignored him, naturally.

But it made me think. With a computer you can send
e-mails.

And Mam works on a computer all the time now, so
she definitely has an e-mail address.

I know we talk on the phone every day, but sometimes
it's easier to write things down than to say them.
Especially when you want to ask tricky questions like
'When am I going to see you again?' and stuff like that.

It's been five months since I've seen her. I wonder if
she looks the same. I know people don't change all that
much in a few months, but still.

Sometimes when I try to see her face in my head I can't, and I have to look at a photo of her to remind myself what she looks like. And that is very scary.

We don't have too many photos of anyone in the house – our camera is embarrassingly old, and nobody is that interested in using it – but we have a video with Mam in it. It's from their tenth wedding anniversary, about five years ago, and some friends of theirs had a surprise party for them in their house, and made a video and gave it to them afterwards.

It says 'Anniversary' on the side of the cassette, and it's probably still sitting on the shelf behind the telly, along with *The Wizard of Oz* and *Chitty Chitty Bang Bang* and Dad's Laurel and Hardy collection, and a few others.

We watched the anniversary video a lot at the start – or at least I did. It was like eavesdropping on Mam and Dad when they were out at night, and I loved it. Mam wore a blue dress with see-through sleeves, and her hands flew up to her face when they walked in the door and all their friends shouted 'Surprise!'. She and Dad looked really happy in the video. They kissed when their friends drank a toast to them.

I might be able to watch it again sometime, but I think I'll stick to the photos for now.

In case you're wondering, here's a description of Mam:

Height:	About 168cm
Hair:	Short and straight, brown but dyed red
Eyes:	Grey
Lipstick:	Rust-coloured, matching her hair

Anything else:	Three holes in one ear, two in the other. A small bump on her nose where she broke it after falling off a horse when she was about my age. A few red lines called broken veins on her cheeks.

She has short, stubby fingers that she hates – she always told me I was lucky I got Dad's hands. She wore a silver ring like a bit of rope on her left little finger, and she smelt of the almond body lotion she put on every morning.

I wonder if she still smells the same. I wonder if her hair is longer, and if she still puts in the red colour every three weeks.

I wonder if she remembers what I look like.

STINKY

STINKY
STINKY
STINKY

Half past seven, the next day.

You are not going to believe this. My father has just gone out with Marjorie Maloney.

Remember her? Lives across the road, dyed black hair, stinky perfume, tight skirts that show her knickers. Breaks her iron so she has an excuse to call over to Dad, and bakes lemon meringue pies that nobody wants.

When Dad told me that he was going out with her this evening, I was sure he was joking. I just looked at him and began to smile, and he said quickly, 'No, really, we are. Just to the cinema, and straight back. Two and a half hours at the most. Will you be OK on your own, or will I get someone to come around?'

I couldn't believe it. He was serious. After all the times we used to hide in the sitting room when she came knocking on the door with one of her yukky casseroles. I thought he felt exactly the same about her as I do.

I was so mad I could hardly talk. I managed to say, 'I don't need a babysitter,' and then I turned and went upstairs, and he had the good sense not to follow me. He called up a few minutes ago to say he was going, and that he'd leave his phone switched on just in case. (Of course HE has a mobile phone, not like some people who've been BEGGING for one for *months*.)

I didn't bother answering him, just turned up Eminem.

I am MAD AS HELL. How DARE he go out with Marjorie Maloney? What if somebody sees them?

As if I'd phone him anyway, even if the house was burning to a cinder. Even if a gang broke in and tied me up and robbed the place. (I know I couldn't phone him if I was tied up, but you know what I mean.)

When I heard the front door closing, I snuck out to the landing and watched him walking across the road to Marjorie Maloney's house. She came out straight away – was probably watching him too, from *her* landing – and they got into his car and drove off, in full view of anyone who might be watching. She had a red skirt and a black top on, and she was giggling like anything as she was getting into his car. I said a quick prayer that she'd catch her skirt in the car door, but God mustn't have been listening.

Half an hour later

OK, I phoned Bumble, who managed to calm me down a bit. He said Marjorie could easily have asked Dad to go out, instead of the other way around, and Dad would be too much of a gentleman to say no, even if it was the last thing he wanted to do.

Bumble also said that maybe Marjorie really wanted to see this film, and maybe there was nobody else to go with her, and she didn't fancy going on her own, so she only asked Dad along to keep her company.

And the more I thought about it, as I was making a peanut butter and banana sandwich afterwards, the less mad I felt. Of course it's not a *date*, nothing like that at all. Dad wouldn't do that, not with Mam only gone a few months. No, he and Marjorie are just sort of friends.

He needs friends, right? Just like me and Bumble.

I don't know what I'd do without Bumble. He's my rock.

I wonder if Mam would ever go to the cinema with another man. She must be meeting lots of new people over there in the States. I don't think I want to think about that right now.

Hope the film is a bummer, even if they are only friends.

SUMMER

SUMMER SUMMER SUMMER SUMMER SUMMER SUMMER SUMMER

Seven o'clock, Tuesday, beginning of June.
Well, summer's here, kind of. Bumble had a pair of shorts on him at school today. Pity his legs are so white and skinny. The rest of him is pretty good – nice light brown hair, green eyes, lovely chuckly laugh that just makes you want to join in. No freckles, not even one. He says I have enough for the two of us, and he's right.

Catherine Eggleston and Terry McNamara are officially going out, which shows what kind of taste *he* has. Although I must admit she's only been about half as bitchy as usual, since I didn't tell on her about the note she wrote that time.

I haven't been sent to Smelly Nelly's for over two weeks, which has to be some kind of record. Not that I care, with less than a month of school to go. Chloe Nelligan is still keeping the vampires away – and the rest of us too – with the dreaded garlic breath.

The only other bit of news is not so good, which is why

I've saved it till last.

Tonight Dad and Marjorie Maloney are going out again, to the launch of some dorky book written by someone Marjorie knows. Dad's in the shower now, getting ready.

But they're *not* dating – Dad's just keeping her company, because she's got nobody else and he feels sorry for her. That's the only possible reason he's doing this. *No way* is he interested in Marjorie Maloney – how could he be, after Mam, who's miles prettier and slimmer?

He did look a bit guilty earlier when he told me he was meeting Marjorie. He tried to make it sound like no big deal: 'By the way, myself and Marjorie are heading out to a book launch tonight, just for a bit.' His back was to me as he spoke, stirring a saucepan, but then he looked around to see how I was taking it. I just nodded, as if I couldn't care less.

Of course Marjorie is acting like my best friend these days, waving at me from across the road any time she sees me. I just ignore her, which makes two people on the road I have to ignore now.

Compared to Marjorie Maloney, Ruth Wallace is a saint. At least she's not trying to get her claws into my dad, just run me over with her wheelchair, or insult me to death.

Bumble's coming over in a while, and we're ordering in a pizza and he's helping me to set up an e-mail account, and I am *not* telling Dad about it. Why should I, when he can just turn around and abandon me any time he feels like it? Bumble says it's dead easy to set up – all we need is a disk that he's bringing over. I just hope the computer is modern enough.

Dad just called in that he's leaving. I called back 'Fine.' I am not going to look out the window this time. I hope the book launch is even more boring than the cinema. I didn't ask him about the film they went to, and he didn't mention it either.

Bumble'd better hurry up, or I'll order the pizza without him. My stomach is beginning to complain of emptiness. We usually get a giant pizza with half of it topped with pepperoni and pineapple for me, and half with ham and mushrooms, for both of us. Well, I'd share my half if he wanted, but pepperoni gives Bumble a rash.

He's getting ten more minutes.

Five to six, Saturday, middle of June.

A funny thing happened today in Boots. I was trying on a lipstick when I saw the girl beside me putting something into her coat pocket. I couldn't see what it was, just that it was small, and then she saw me looking, and she turned and walked away really quickly.

It was the first time I'd ever seen anyone shoplifting.

I didn't know whether I should tell someone, but then I figured by the time I did she'd be long gone. And it looked so small, whatever she'd taken. It must have been a lipstick or something. Probably cost less than five euros.

She was just about my age too, or maybe a bit older. One of her eyebrows was pierced, which I think looks so cool.

It looked dead easy, what she did. Nobody saw a thing except me, and she was gone in a second. One free lipstick in her pocket.

Not that I'd ever do it – I'd be terrified of being caught. And just imagine what Mr Grouchy would say then. I'd probably be sent to my room for ten years.

God, I'm so hungry. Dad's cooking has not improved with practice. The only good thing is he's given up making porridge for the summer, and now we have Weetabix for breakfast. But dinners are still pretty bad.

Sausages are classic – they're always burnt on one side and raw on the other. When he grills fish fingers, they're as dry as a bone. And he can NOT heat up baked beans without letting half of them stick to the pot. Can you believe it? But we order in quite a lot too, like Chinese or pizza, which we never did when Mam was here, and which suits me fine.

I've got a few new spots on my chin, that Bumble says is probably from all the takeaway food I've been eating, but I don't listen – he has at least three more spots than me. He says that his ones are normal teenage spots, even though they look exactly the same as mine.

Ruth Wallace told me I was getting fat the last time I saw her. She didn't even notice the spots. She's such an idiot.

Mam and I are e-mailing now. I can't believe how easy it is. My typing is a bit slow, but who cares? The great thing is, Mam is just getting into work when I get home from school, so she's sitting right there at her computer when I send her a message, and she often e-mails me right back. It makes her feel closer somehow.

And it's not that I'm deceiving Dad – I'm just not telling him about it, which is a completely different thing. He'd only worry about me using the Internet, in case some weirdo tried to make contact with me, or something. So it's best for everyone, if he doesn't know.

Remember I told you that Mam's sharing a flat with a couple called George and Enda? Well it turns out that they're two men – my mother is living with two gay men. Is that weird, or what? She says they're great, very tidy and both excellent cooks. We could sure use one of them around here sometimes.

I haven't asked her yet about when she's coming home to see me. I thought it would be easier on the computer, but it isn't. What if she says it could be ages? At least if I don't know, I can go on hoping she'll come back really soon, maybe even for good. I wish she'd mention it herself though.

The only bad thing is I can't print out her e-mails, because we don't have a printer, and I'm afraid to save them in case Dad finds them. I know Bumble says nobody can read my e-mails without knowing my password, but as Granny Daly would say, *BETTER SAFE THAN SORRY.*

By the way, before you ask – yes, Marjorie Maloney is still Dad's new best friend. They've been out four times now. See if I care. As long as he NEVER, EVER brings her home here afterwards.

I haven't mentioned Marjorie to Mam. Well, there's no point, is there? Anyway, we've got more important things to talk about, like Enda and George, who both work in a gym, and who've got Mam cheap membership there. And about the haircut I got last week that Bumble says makes me look a lot older.

It's much sunnier in San Francisco than in Ireland, except around Christmas when it can get a bit chilly and wet, but it's foggy there too, near the ocean – that's the Pacific Ocean, on the other side of America. Mam says the area she lives in is called the sunny Mission, because it's hardly ever foggy there.

I'd love to go and visit her. Maybe I could save up my pocket money for a trip, ha ha. I'm not exactly the most well paid teenager in town. Dad says you don't need a lot of money to enjoy yourself, which goes to show how out of touch he is. I bet everyone in my class gets more pocket money than me. I bet Catherine Eggleston gets loads.

She and Trudy Higgins have fake tans, which Bumble and I think is very sad. Terry McNamara probably likes it – he and Catherine are still MADLY IN LOVE. Someone get me a bucket, quick.

Right, Dad just shouted up that dinner is ready. Tonight we're having roast chicken, so if you don't hear from me again it's probably because I died of salmonella poisoning.

to: STUPID
cc: STUPID
bcc: STUPID
subject: STUPID

stupid stupid stupid stupid stupid stupid stupid stupid stu
stupid stupid stupid stupid stupid stupid stupid stupid stu
stupid stupid stupid stupid stupid stupid stupid stupid stu
stupid stupid stupid stupid stupid stupid stupid stupid stu
stupid stupid stupid stupid stupid stupid stupid stupid stu
stupid stupid stupid stupid stupid stupid stupid stupid stu

Ten past five, Tuesday, still middle of June.

OK, Dad's mad at me again, and it's my own stupid fault.

You know how I've been e-mailing Mam without him knowing? Well, yesterday I was just signing off when the doorbell rang, and it was a woman with a clipboard, asking if I wanted to do a survey about eating habits, which, of course, I couldn't resist.

I told her that there were ten people living in the house, and that eight of us were allergic to vegetables. I told her that I had popcorn and yoghurt for breakfast, and that my favourite treat was pickled rhubarb, and that one of my brothers would only eat food that was yellow. It was lots of fun.

I'm not sure how much she believed, but she wrote it all down, and thanked me very politely at the end. After she was gone, I went upstairs to do some painting, and totally forgot that the phone line was still plugged into the back of the computer. Bad mistake.

Of course Dad went to make a phone call about ten minutes after he got home, and discovered my mistake. So then we had the Big Investigation, with him standing there like someone out of the Secret Service, and talking about going behind his back, and how could he trust me again, and stuff like that. And of course he went on about the dangers of the Internet, like I knew he would.

And I'm sure I could still have got away with it if I'd played along, told him how sorry I was, and how I just wanted to keep in touch with Mam in as many ways as I could, and promised him that I wasn't surfing the net looking for porn, and he probably would have huffed and puffed a bit, and then given in and agreed to let me keep emailing.

But, of course, I didn't do the sensible thing at all. I told him I had to go behind his back, because I knew he wouldn't let me get an e-mail address, because he was such a meanie, and it was my right to use a computer if I wanted, especially if he was going to go off with the first woman who looked at him.

And as soon as I said that last bit, I knew I'd gone too far. He pressed his lips together and walked over to the computer and plugged it out, and told me that he was bringing it back to work in the morning, since clearly I couldn't be trusted with it.

God, he is *such* a pain. Imagine I ever thought I'd miss him, if I'd gone off with Mam.

But the joke's on him, because there's an Internet café in town that he probably doesn't even know about, and I can call there on my way home from school, and keep on e-mailing Mam, and anyone else I want (although the only other person whose e-mail address I know is Bumble, and I don't think I'd have much to say to him, seeing as how we're together every day for about five hours.)

And since Dad is now convinced that I can't be trusted, I've nothing to lose if I feel like doing something really bad – which is kind of exciting.

Let's see what really bad thing I can think of.

love,

STUPID

TROUBLE AGAIN

Twenty to seven, Monday, beginning of last week of June.
I've really done it now – I'm in the biggest trouble of my
life. And you know what the worst bit is? It wasn't even
fun.

Here's what happened. I was walking out of Boots this
afternoon when I felt a hand on my shoulder. I turned
around and this woman said, 'I need you to come back
inside with me now.'

I looked at her with my most innocent face and asked
her why, but she just took me by the elbow and sort of
marched me back inside, and I thought it might be
better not to make a fuss so I went with her, hoping she
couldn't hear my thumping heart.

She wasn't wearing a uniform, just a normal jumper
and skirt, so if anyone saw us I could say afterwards
that she was my aunt, or something. At least, that's
what I thought then. Anyway, she brought me into a
small room and sat me down, and asked me to empty

the pockets of my school blazer, which I did, since I hadn't really any choice.

I took out a comb and a lipstick and half a pack of wine gums and my wallet and a small bottle of shampoo, the travel size, and I put them all on the desk between us. She picked up the bottle of shampoo, which was the only thing that looked like it was new, and she asked me if I'd paid for it, which was a pretty dumb question, considering that she knew well that I hadn't.

So I just sat there and said nothing, and did my best to look bored, even though I was pretty scared. My first time shoplifting, and I had to be caught. I wondered what prison food tasted like.

Yes, I stole the shampoo. I know I said I'd be too terrified, but I was so mad at Dad after the whole computer thing, I just decided that it might be a bit of a laugh if I could get away with it. I didn't think too much about what might happen if I was caught.

To make a long story short, Dad was called from work to come and get me, and I knew as soon as I saw his face that I was in big trouble. He spoke very politely to the woman and apologised for his terrible daughter (he didn't actually say terrible, but I knew he was thinking it). The woman said they wouldn't press charges, since this was my first offence, but that she would be contacting the school to let them know.

Bugger, bugger, bugger.

I hadn't told Bumble what I was planning – one of the few things I kept from him. I kind of knew this was one thing he wouldn't go along with. But now Smelly Nelly is going to find out – and what if she says it to Chloe? I can just imagine the fun Catherine Eggleston and Trudy Higgins will have if they ever get to hear about this.

To be fair to Dad, he did his best to persuade the woman not to inform the school. He said I was about to start secondary school, and it would be a blot on my character if they heard about this, and he was sure I'd learnt my lesson now, and other stuff like that. But the woman wouldn't agree not to tell the school. She said they treated shoplifting as a very serious offence, and I had to be made an example of. In the end, Dad gave up.

He didn't open his mouth on the way home, and I thought it was probably a good idea to say nothing either, so it sure was a quiet journey. As soon as we got inside the house, though, he made up for it. He asked me if I was trying to end up in jail. He told me he was shocked and disappointed in me, said I only had to ask if I needed more pocket money.

He went on like this for about ten minutes, and even though he didn't get mad at me, like he'd done with the computer business, I knew he was really upset. His face was white and pinched looking, and his voice was tight, as if he was trying hard not to lose his temper. And somehow, it was much worse than if he'd shouted at me.

Just as he was winding down, the phone rang, and he said, 'You'd better answer it,' and it was really hard to talk to Mam and not tell her what happened – which of course I couldn't. Imagine what *she'd* say. Luckily she couldn't stay long on the phone, because she was on her way to a meeting.

After I hung up, Dad came out of the kitchen and sent me upstairs and said he'd bring up something to eat later. Something tells me it won't be a pepperoni and pineapple pizza.

And you know what? It wasn't even the right kind of shampoo – it was one for greasy hair, which I don't have. I only noticed that when it was sitting on the store detective's desk. That's kind of funny, when you think about it.

Although I don't really feel like laughing right now.

Later

You will *not* believe what just happened. There was a tap at the door and I ignored it, and then it opened and MARJORIE MALONEY walked in holding a plate. I just looked at her, totally gobsmacked. I think my mouth might have dropped open like some goofy fish, but I'm not sure.

She stood inside the door with a goody-goody face on her, and said in a nun's voice, 'Liz, is it OK if we have a chat?' Can you imagine? Me and Marjorie Maloney, bonding. AS IF.

So of course I told her it was definitely NOT OK, and to kindly leave my room, which she didn't do.

She put the plate down on my dressing table – not one of our plates – and she said, 'Liz, I know how you feel ...' and I interrupted, because I couldn't bear to listen to her, and I told her she *didn't* know how I felt, she hadn't a *clue* how I felt, and to LEAVE ME ALONE. And then I turned my back on her and listened to the door closing quietly when she went out.

I can NOT believe that he got her to come up to my room. I can't believe he did that. If he thinks I'm going to touch her crummy plate of food, he's got another think coming.

It sure smells good, though, and I'm starving. I've had nothing to eat since a Nutella sandwich at half twelve, and it's well after seven now. But nothing in this world would make me touch Marjorie Maloney's food.

Anyway, I can't see what it is, because there's one of those silver lids on top that you get in hotels sometimes. Marjorie Maloney, trying to be posh. It's pathetic.

Ten to eight

It was some kind of fish pie. I left it as long as I could, so it wasn't that hot any more, but I was so hungry I didn't care. But I'm still MAD at Dad for getting that woman involved in our private affairs.

As if she was part of our family, which she never, NEVER will be.

If I still had that fiver she gave me for my birthday, I'd throw it back at her and tell her what she could do with her crummy money.

Hey, I've just thought of a new name for her: Marjorie Baloney.

God, I HATE the thought of school in the morning. Maybe Smelly Nelly will announce at assembly that we have a thief in our midst, or something. What a dope I am sometimes.

Bedtime, last day of primary school, ever.

I can't understand the way I feel today. I thought I'd be on top of the world – no more Santa, no more visits to Smelly Nelly's office – but I'm not. I'm lonely and sad, and I miss everyone like mad already, even though I'll probably meet most of them around town over the summer.

Isn't it funny? All through sixth class, we couldn't wait to be finished with primary school. We counted down the days since Easter, and moaned and groaned about how bored we were – and now that it's finished at last, there's just this giant empty space.

And now we're going from being the oldest kids in school, the ones in charge, to being the youngest – that'll be really strange.

Mam says she remembers feeling exactly the same. I e-mail her from the Internet café most days now on the way home from school, and usually she answers me back straight away. The great thing is I can print off her mails, which I couldn't do at home. I have a bundle of them in my knicker drawer, the only place I can be sure Dad won't go near, ha ha.

Of course I didn't tell her about being caught shoplifting – but the good news is that Smelly Nelly didn't tell anyone about it either. She did call me into her office, the day after it happened, but for once I didn't try to be smart, or look bored or whatever. I sat quietly and listened to her saying all the same kind of things that Dad had said to me the day before, and then I told her that I'd definitely learnt my lesson, and would never do it again.

And she smiled at me and shook my hand, and said she believed me, which for some weird reason made me feel really good. I know Smelly and I haven't always been the best of friends, especially since Mam left, but right then, she was OK. She wished me luck in secondary school, and she said she hoped I'd keep making the most of my artistic talent, and that she knew I'd go far. Imagine.

And now it's three days later, and we had our graduation ceremony in the hall this afternoon, and Dad was there along with all the other parents, and loads of them had brought along camcorders and cameras, and it was like the Oscars.

And naturally Catherine Eggleston was in floods of tears, but I have to say she wasn't the only one. Everyone was passing around autograph books, or just copies, and getting e-mail addresses and phone numbers.

It just feels very weird right now. Tomorrow Bumble and I are going into town to meet up with a few of the others for lunch. Wonder if we'll all drift apart, when we're scattered in different schools.

Not Bumble and me, of course, even though he's going to the Comprehensive and I'm going to St Rita's. We'll be best friends forever, even if we end up living on opposite sides of the world. But guess what? The only other person who's going with me to St Rita's is Chloe Nelligan – can you believe it? Old garlic breath Chloe. I'll have to practise breathing through my mouth until I make new friends.

I think I need some ice cream now. If I sneak past the sitting room Dad won't hear.

Seven o'clock, Saturday, middle of July.

It was SO hot today. We went to the seaside, me and Dad and Bumble. Yesterday was Bumble's thirteenth birthday. I got him a faded grey t-shirt in Next that I knew he liked, and he wore it today.

My nose is burnt, because I forgot to bring sunscreen with me. When we dropped Bumble home, his Mam gave me a little tub of natural yoghurt to put on my nose, but it seemed such a waste of good food. I love yoghurt, especially with a banana chopped into it. Luckily, we had one banana left at home.

One good thing is that Marjorie Baloney has kept her distance since the whole shoplifting business. She and Dad still go out, usually on Friday nights, but she hasn't been around to our house since that day, which suits me just fine, and Dad never mentions her. He'll probably get sick of her any day now, and that'll be the end of that.

Dad only goes into work in the mornings while I'm on holidays. In the afternoons, he works from home, on the computer that he brought back home again. He said nothing when he carried it into the house, and neither did I. I haven't gone near it, even when he's out at work in the mornings. Who needs it now?

I can't believe I'll be starting secondary school in a month and a bit. It'll be the first time Bumble and I won't be together since Junior Infants.

That was where we met. We were sitting beside one another on our first day at school, and I hit him and made him cry when he broke one of my crayons, and I was put sitting on a chair facing the wall, and the next day he gave me a new box of crayons that his mam bought when he told her what happened, and we've been best friends ever since.

Of course we'll still meet after school and at weekends and stuff, but I'm a bit afraid it won't be the same. He'll probably start hanging around with boys now, and maybe he'll be ashamed to be seen with me, so we'll have to meet in secret.

Or maybe I'll have to disguise myself as a boy. I've been practising making my voice lower, just in case. Bumble's voice was the first to break in the class, just after we went into sixth, and he got an awful slagging from the other boys. I bet it was because they were jealous that Bumble sounded all grown up, and they were still talking like girls.

And now Chris Thompson is the only one whose voice still hasn't broken. Hopefully he's not in a hurry to get a girlfriend. Maybe some girls wouldn't mind having a boyfriend with the same kind of voice as them, although I have to say I'd be a bit embarrassed.

But apart from his voice, there's nothing wrong with Chris – he's easily the cutest-looking guy from our old class, with greenish-brown eyes and lovely floppy, dark blonde hair, and a gorgeous dimple in one cheek when he smiles, much nicer than my horrible chin dimple.

And really straight teeth too, once his braces came off.

Next week I'm going to be fitted for my new school uniform. It's brown and cream, not that colours really matter when you're talking about a school uniform – they're not exactly the height of fashion. My old one was blue, and just as boring. I'm going to see if Dad will spring for a new pair of shoes too, even though I got some in May. Maybe he's forgotten.

It's usually pretty easy to get money from Dad for stuff – I just tell him I have to buy girl's things, and he gets his wallet out really quickly and asks how much I need. You can guess what he thinks I'm getting.

I have to tell you – Ruth Wallace was wearing the dorkiest hat I ever saw yesterday. It was bright orange with a fat red stripe going through the middle of it. It looked like a baboon's bottom sitting on her head. I didn't say that, of course, not even when she made puking noises as I passed her.

What a moron she is. I am not going anywhere near Wallaces until this nose calms down. Imagine the fun she'd have with it.

It's really stinging now. Pity I ate all that yoghurt. Maybe I've got sunstroke. Can you die of that? Imagine if Dad came in here in the morning, wondering why I wasn't getting up for breakfast, and found me stretched out on the floor, deathly pale except for a bright red nose.

You'd think he'd have remembered the sun cream. Mam would have – and she'd have had natural yogurt too.

When Mam lived here, our fridge was always full of healthy food like cottage cheese and cucumbers and broccoli. Now we have things like salami and smoked mackerel and tubs of duck pate, which Dad loves, and big jars of crunchy peanut butter and Nutella for me.

And we eat white bread, which Mam never bought. She said it was rubbish, even the kind with the seeds and stuff in it.

And these days there's always at least one tub of Ben & Jerry's in the freezer. When Mam lived with us, we'd get Ben & Jerry's once in a blue moon, only on very special occasions. And the funny thing is, I'm not half as mad about it now as I was then. I mean, I still eat it, quite a lot actually, but somehow it's not the treat it used to be.

Funny, isn't it?

And when Mam was here, she stuck things like bin collection times and dentist appointments and the plumber's emergency number on the front of the fridge. Now it's covered with takeaway menus, all our favourite ones. I wonder where all the other stuff went. Maybe it's still there, under the menus.

Not that I'm bothered. I just wonder, that's all.

Way past bedtime, Sunday, 31st August.

God, I can't believe summer's over. Tomorrow I start secondary school, and I just know I'm not going to sleep a wink. I'm scared stiff, to tell you the truth. Just hope Chloe Nelligan is there before me.

I'm getting a bus to school, because it's too far to walk, and Dad's work is in the opposite direction. Mam or Dad always brought me to primary school, so this'll be my first time on a school bus. I won't know a single person on it.

What if they pick on the new people? What if there's one horrible bully on it who decides that I look like a good target? What if I do something stupid, like get my bag tangled in the seat, or trip or something, and they all laugh? What if someone sticks chewing gum in my hair?

This is so horrible. I wish Mam was here. I hate her for going. No, I don't mean that – of course I don't hate her. But I sure wish she was here.

I'm meeting Bumble after school, so we can compare notes. It's OK for him – loads of people from our old class are going to the Comp, so he'll have plenty of pals. Why am I going to stupid St Rita's?

I never thought I'd be looking forward to meeting Chloe.

I've started biting my nails again. Bugger. I hadn't done it all summer, and they were just beginning to look really good. Now they're all raggy again.

Ten to nine, Monday, 1st September.

Well, that wasn't too bad.

The bus was OK. I had to sit beside someone because it was quite full, so I picked a quiet-looking girl with the same colour hair as Mam, and then I pretended to be really interested in my new science book for the whole journey. She must have thought I was a right swot, ha ha.

Chloe Nelligan was in the yard. She came straight up to me when I walked off the bus, and boy was I glad to see her. I hardly even noticed the garlic breath. She looked just as scared as I felt. We chatted until the bell rang – she was in the Isle of Man for the whole month of July, staying with cousins – and then we were brought into the hall where the principal met us and gave us a talk, and after that we were split into groups and shown around the school.

The art room is brilliant. Imagine, a room especially

for painting. I can't wait to get in there. We've double art on Thursdays, hurrah. Wonder what the teacher's like – we didn't get to meet her because she was teaching another class, but she looked OK.

We've got a form teacher, which means she'll be sort of like our minder – if we've got any problems we can go to her. Her name's Mrs Keogh, and she seems really nice and friendly. And there are two sixth-year prefects in charge of our class too, like we used to look after the Junior Infants sometimes in primary.

Some of the sixth years look like proper grown-ups. Imagine I'll be like that in five years' time. It's kind of scary and kind of exciting at the same time.

When I got home from school there was a letter from San Francisco waiting for me, which turned out to be a Good Luck card from Mam with a $50 note inside it. I really miss her. It seems like forever since we met.

Bumble was late, as usual, but it was because he was signing up for the after-school soccer club. He says the Comp is brilliant. They have their own swimming pool, which I'm dead jealous about. He's in the same class as Chris Thompson (remember the one with the girly voice?) and Terry McNamara, who's still going out with Catherine Eggleston. She's going to the Comp too, but she was put into a different class. The dunces' one probably, ha ha.

Anyway, I think secondary school is going to be OK after all.

Wonder how many euros I'll get for $50. There's a really cool top in River Island that I might try on tomorrow.

AND COUNTING

3

Tomorrow is Dad's birthday. He'll be thirty-six, I think. I was going to get him a bottle of the aftershave he always uses, when I realised that it would make him smell nice for Marjorie Baloney, so I didn't. He's getting a book token now, which is really far more useful.

I'm sure he'd love to read a book, if the newspaper didn't take him so long every day. He'll have plenty of time for reading during the Christmas holidays, when he's off work.

Can you believe that he's still meeting Marjorie? Even though I'm pretty sure they're just friends, it's still a bit embarrassing, at their age. I'm not sure how old Marjorie is, but I'm willing to bet she's at least thirty-six. Probably a lot more. I bet that's why she dyes her hair, to disguise the grey.

Mam did not have one single bit of grey – that was definitely NOT the reason *she* coloured her hair. And

Mam's looked really natural anyway, not a bit fake.

I haven't seen Bumble since the first day of school, but we've been on the phone a lot. At least, I've been ringing him a lot – he isn't great at phoning, which I suppose is typical of boys. He says he really likes the Comp. He says they get lots of homework, especially science, but he's good at that, so he doesn't really mind.

It's kind of cool to have different teachers for every subject. A lot better than having to look at Santa all day long, with his wonky eyes and red-haired ears. We have a lovely teacher for English and social studies called Miss Purtill. She's youngish, only about twenty-three or four I'd say, and she's got bobbed blonde hair and grey eyes, and she has real classy clothes that you know didn't come from Penney's.

She smells great too – sort of flowery, but not too strong. And her nails are always perfectly done. (I've stopped biting mine again, by the way. We're allowed nail varnish in this school, so I'm going to get a bottle of pearly pink, like Miss Purtill wears. It's so feminine.)

So anyway, I've decided that Miss Purtill is just what Dad needs to get him away from Marjorie – which is why I've been mentioning her a lot at home (Miss Purtill obviously, not Marjorie). I've been saying what a great teacher she is too, so he'll be going in to see her with a really positive attitude.

And next to art, English is my best subject – I've always got high marks in it. And everyone does well at social studies; it's just that kind of subject, so Miss Purtill will be giving Dad a good report. The more I think about it, the more certain I am that Dad will ask her out to dinner or something, and that'll be the end of him and Marjorie Baloney.

Now I'd better stop. I have an essay on the War of Independence to finish, and history is far from my best subject, so it's going to take quite a while.

Oh by the way, I'm planning to cook Dad a birthday dinner on Friday night, which should be interesting, as I've never really cooked a full meal on my own before.

After dinner, Friday, 12th September.

I am NEVER cooking anything ever again. It was a total and utter *disaster*.

I decided to do Hawaiian Pork Chops, because they sounded dead easy – just chops with pineapple rings sitting on top of them. Except that I bought pineapple pieces instead of rings by mistake, so I tried to join the pieces together to make circles, which was very messy and not all that successful. The chops got a bit burnt too, while I was trying to make swans out of the serviettes. I covered the black parts with pineapple pieces, but it didn't make them taste any better.

Dad was great. He said it all tasted wonderful, and he ate every bit of his chop, even the fat, which I thought was really nice of him. He ate some of the rice too, even though it was extremely salty because I thought 'tsp' meant tablespoon instead of teaspoon.

Dad sure drank loads of water.

At least the dessert was OK – baked apples in the microwave with a dollop of Ben & Jerry's on top. You can't really go wrong with dessert as long as Ben & Jerry's is in there somewhere.

Dad and Marjorie Baloney are going out to dinner tomorrow night, and I suppose whatever they get will be a lot tastier than burnt pork chops with broken pineapple rings on top, but as Granny Daly would say, *IT'S THE THOUGHT THAT COUNTS.*

Marjorie gave Dad a silver photo frame for his birthday, which I thought showed very little imagination. I was going to suggest that he put a photo of the family in there – meaning one of him, Mam and me – but then I decided it would be more mature just to ignore it. He hasn't put anything into it yet anyway, which is a big relief.

I can't wait till he meets Miss Purtill.

I'm still pretending not to see Marjorie across the street now, although she always waves over at me. She doesn't even notice that I'm ignoring her. Some people are so unobservant.

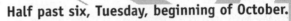

Half past six, Tuesday, beginning of October.
Bumble is auditioning for the part of Danny in *Grease* – that's the Christmas show the Comp is putting on. I've offered to help him with his lines, but so far he hasn't asked me. Imagine I never knew Bumble could sing. Actually I can't imagine him hip-hopping to 'Summer Loving', but I do hope he gets the part – it would be cool to see him onstage at Christmas.

I'm not sure how I feel about Christmas this year. Everything is bound to remind Dad and me of Mam, since she was here for all the other ones. And we always used to hang the decorations on the tree together – it was kind of a family tradition.

We'd wait till Dad got home from work, and I'd do the low down ones and Mam would be in the middle and Dad would do the high bits, and at the end Dad would lift me up and I'd hang the star on top, and then Mam would make hot chocolate with marshmallows, and we'd play Pictionary while we drank it, and I'd win and Dad would come last. It was always the same, every year.

I can't believe it's almost a year since I've seen Mam. She hasn't mentioned coming back to Ireland for Christmas – maybe she's planning to surprise me.

And of course we won't have Granny Daly either. She's been coming to us every Christmas for years, since Grandad Daly died. Surely Mam would want to see her mother at Christmas.

I wish I could pluck up the courage to ask her if she's coming home, but I can't. It's the only thing I can't talk to her about.

Well, that and Marjorie, of course.

And the shoplifting.

And all the visits to Smelly Nelly's office.

And the fact that Dad didn't know I was e-mailing her.

Gee, I didn't realise there were so many things that I don't talk to Mam about.

Anyway, back to Christmas. Dad's parents live in Australia. They emigrated years ago, before I was born, and they've only been back twice, both times in the spring. They never fly home at Christmas because it's too crowded, and the fares are too high.

So it looks like it'll be just Dad and me for Christmas dinner. I wonder which one of us will cook the turkey – or should I say burn the turkey. We'll probably do it together, so we can blame each other when it's a disaster.

It might surprise you to hear that I've got quite friendly with Chloe Nelligan at school. She's actually not bad, I've discovered. Once you get used to the garlic breath, she's quite funny and clever.

We're in the same group for a science project, and she's come up with some really good ideas. Imagine I was in her class for eight years and I never really noticed her. And I suppose she can't help it if her mother or father, or whoever cooks the dinner in that house, puts garlic into everything.

I actually went over to her house the other night to work on the science project, and it was really weird to have Smelly Nelly bringing us milk and biscuits, like she was just a normal mother. I mean, of course she is a normal mother to Chloe, but I couldn't help still thinking of her as a principal, and remembering all my visits to her office. Not that she mentioned them of course – she just treated me like any friend of Chloe's and said she loved my hair, and told me that she'd always wanted curly hair when she was a girl.

It was a bit creepy really – and you know what else? I didn't get any smell of garlic in the house, which was very weird, considering that they must use it by the bucketful. But Chloe's OK.

Oh, and guess who I saw in town today – Chris Thompson. Remember him, cutest guy in sixth class? He looks just as nice as ever. I didn't talk to him – he was across the road, so we just waved at each other. I'd forgotten what a gorgeous smile he has.

Well, time for some homework, I suppose. Can't put it off forever. Only two weeks to the mid term break – not that I'm counting.

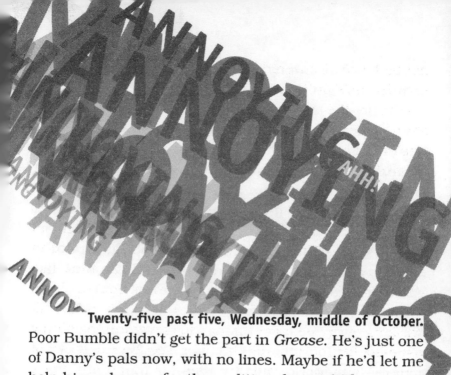

Twenty-five past five, Wednesday, middle of October.
Poor Bumble didn't get the part in *Grease*. He's just one
of Danny's pals now, with no lines. Maybe if he'd let me
help him rehearse for the audition, he might have done
better, but of course I didn't say that.

I haven't seen him for ages, and talking on the phone is
just not the same. I miss him.

I'm really glad I've got Chloe now though.

And wouldn't you know – Catherine Eggleston got the
part of Sandy, with her blonde hair and her boobs.
Naturally, she was the first girl to get boobs in our
class. I'm still as flat as a pancake, which I'm sure is
perfectly normal for most thirteen-year-olds. Chloe
wears a bra, but as far as I can see it's really just for
show.

Oh, and guess what else? Bumble told me it's all
finished between Catherine and Terry McNamara. I'm
glad Terry came to his senses at last. And guess who

got the part of Danny? Cute Chris Thompson, which I suppose means that his voice has finally broken – they could hardly have a Danny with a high voice, could they? The songs would sound all wrong.

And more news – Pizza Palace, which Dad and I use all the time, has a new delivery boy, and he really *does* look Italian, not like Santa – remember my old teacher?

This guy has dark brown eyes and long black hair that he wears in a really cool ponytail, and he calls me 'doll'. He must be at least seventeen, because he rides one of the Pizza Palace motorbikes. I would give ANYTHING to go out with him.

Oh, and I almost forgot – I was at Dad's office last week. We were going to have an early bird dinner at the Chinese, so I got the bus to his place from school and did my homework while I waited for him – and guess what was on his desk? The silver frame that Marjorie gave him for his birthday.

When I saw it, I was half afraid to look at what he'd put into it, in case it was a photo of her and him, but it turned out to be one of me and Bumble from that day on the beach when I burnt my nose, with Bumble making rabbit ears behind my head.

I thought it was nice of Dad to put that photo in, although it made me sad to think we'll never have any new ones of Mam and us.

Ruth Wallace told me my new platforms made me walk like a duck. She's such an idiot.

Two days to mid-term – hurrah! Not that I'm planning anything very exciting, but it'll be great to have a week off. I can stay in bed till – well, till bedtime, if I like, ha ha.

Half eleven, Monday, around the start of November.
What a horrible day. It started out OK, but it got
horrible very quickly.

Here's what happened. I got to school as usual, and I
was catching up with Chloe's news, because we were
just back after mid-term, and her family had gone to
their holiday cottage in Kerry for the week.

Then, right in the middle of her telling me about this
gorgeous guy in the next cottage, I got this awful pain,
down low in my stomach. It was like something twisting
around the wrong way, and it made me double up, it
was so bad.

I never felt anything like it before. I thought it was my
appendix bursting, and if I hadn't been in such pain I
would have been imagining Dad rushing to the hospital
where I was undergoing emergency surgery, and maybe
even Mam flying home to be at my bedside.

Anyway, Chloe left me curled up in the yard and ran

to get a teacher because she was sure I was dying, and by the time she came back with Mrs O'Keefe who teaches maths and geography I was able to stand up a bit, but I still felt pretty gross, and my back was starting to hurt too.

Mrs O'Keefe said I looked very pale, and wondered if it was something I'd eaten, and asked me what I'd had for dinner the night before. I told her bacon and cabbage, because I was too embarrassed to say lamb korma with potato bhajis and naan bread.

Then the pain in my stomach got bad again, and Mrs O'Keefe sent Chloe in to the secretary's office to get her to phone Dad at work and tell him to come and get me. I was doubled up again like an old woman. Everyone around me was staring. I would have been mortified, if I wasn't too busy trying not to die.

When I could move a bit, Mrs O'Keefe helped me into the lobby and sat me on a couch to wait for Dad. I had to sit crouched over with my arms wrapped around my middle, and my face was cold and felt sweaty, and that awful twisting feeling kept coming and going in my stomach.

The secretary made me a cup of tea, which I tried really hard to drink so I wouldn't hurt her feelings, but it was weak and milky and not half sweet enough, and the most I could manage was two or three sips.

You'll get an idea of how rotten I felt, when I tell you that the thought of missing double history, which was first thing after break on Monday, did nothing to cheer me up.

By the time Dad arrived I was feeling a tiny bit better,

so we decided that he'd bring me home and we'd wait a while to see if I needed the doctor. It was only when I got home and went to the bathroom that I discovered what was wrong. At least I was glad it wasn't my appendix about to burst all over the place.

I knew all about periods since fifth class. A woman came to the school one day and took the girls and boys off in separate groups, and showed us some seriously embarrassing posters, and packs of sanitary towels and stuff.

And the boys sure were quiet when they came back from *their* talk, which made a pleasant change.

So I understood what was happening, but now I had a pretty big problem, because I had no stuff. I hadn't bought any sanitary towels, and of course Dad hadn't either. That was definitely the kind of thing mams did. So I managed the best I could with some toilet paper and then I went downstairs, still holding on to my stomach, which was twisting away like mad again, and I told Dad that I needed him to go and get me some sanitary towels.

I was totally mortified – could hardly look at him – but I had to tell someone, and he was all I had. And I'm sure he was just as mortified.

He swallowed a bit and sort of mumbled, 'OK, go and lie down and I'll sort it out.' So I hobbled back upstairs and just waited, curled up with my arms wrapped around my legs because that was the only position that I could bear. I was sorry I hadn't filled a hot water bottle when I was downstairs, but it seemed like too much trouble to go down again.

And about twenty minutes later there was a knock at the door, and when I said, 'Come in,' the door opened and in walked Marjorie Baloney.

And I have to be totally honest here and say that I was kind of glad to see her.

Only because she was female, of course, and because this was the kind of thing that really needed a female.

She looked at me with a kind of worried smile on her face, and said, 'You poor thing,' and then she pulled a packet of sanitary towels out of a bag she was carrying. I just took them and legged it to the bathroom, and when I came back to my room a few minutes later she was gone.

But there was a hot water bottle in my bed, and in the bag she left behind I found a bunch of magazines, a big bar of Dairy Milk, a packet of Tylenol and two cans of ginger ale. Oh, and a bar of White Musk soap. How did she know I liked White Musk?

So now I'm sitting in bed with the hot water bottle pressed to my stomach, which has calmed down a lot. I do feel a bit sick, but that's probably because I've eaten three-quarters of the bar of Dairy Milk and drunk all the ginger ale.

When I've finished reading the magazines, I'll be able to trade them at school.

Maybe I won't call her Marjorie Baloney any more. That was kind of nice, what she did today. And I suppose I'll have to stop pretending not to see her across the road.

But she is still not getting my Dad – no way. The parent-teacher meetings are on next week, and I'm pretty sure Dad and Miss Purtill will like each other.

Not that I want him to end up with *her* either, though – I just don't want him to get stuck with the same friend all the time. It's good for him to get out of the house now and again, and if he took turns with Marjorie and Miss Purtill, then neither of them could get the wrong idea.

My stomach has just started cramping again. Being a woman sucks. Maybe if I finish off the chocolate it'll help.

Bet Ruth Wallace hasn't started her period yet. She's such a baby.

V.GO

GOOD

Five past seven, Tuesday, beginning of December.
OK, first the good news. I got great reports from all the teachers at the parent-teacher meetings. Even Mr O'Connor who teaches history, and who keeps telling me that I'll never make a historian, said I was a very likeable and outgoing girl, which I thought was really nice of him, since that was probably the only positive thing he could think of to say about me. I'm really going to try harder at history now.

The not-so-good news is that I don't think Dad took much notice of Miss Purtill. He didn't look as if he had anything to hide when he got home; he didn't look particularly excited or anything. I asked him what he thought of all the teachers, and he just said they were OK, and I seemed to be doing fine, and then he gave me ten euros. He was probably relieved that I'm not getting hauled into the principal's office any more.

And Miss Purtill didn't treat me any differently the

next day at school, didn't mention Dad to me at all, even though I hung around after her class especially to give her a chance.

So I suppose that's that – my big plan failed.

Marjorie Maloney's hair is now light brown. It's certainly an improvement on the black. Actually, I think it makes her look a lot younger. Not that I'd ever mention that to Dad, of course. They're still going out every weekend, which makes it almost six months now. It looks like I'll just have to live with it, as long as they don't try to change anything.

I say 'hello' now if I meet her on the street, but that's as far as it goes. No chatting, absolutely not. There is no need to give her any ideas about becoming friends with me, just because she helped me out once.

Chloe usually comes around to my house on the nights Dad goes out, not Bumble any more. They both came once, after I started hanging around with Chloe at school, and it was a disaster. Bumble said he nearly passed out, stuck on the couch between the garlic and the White Musk.

And Chloe went all quiet, like she used to when we were in primary school. Maybe she was remembering what it was like when no one really hung around with her. I wonder if she thought it was because she was the principal's daughter. Maybe I should tell her it was just the garlic breath.

Although the funny thing is, I hardly notice it any more.

I haven't seen too much of Bumble at all since the summer. It sure makes me feel sad. I thought we'd never stop being friends.

I'll meet him next week though, when Chloe and I go to the show, and I'm looking forward to meeting up with some of our old classmates too, although I get the impression that Chloe isn't that pushed really – I mean, she wants to see the show, but I don't think there's anyone from our old class that she's dying to meet again.

Funny, how you can miss some things completely. There was me, feeling so lonely when Mam left, and there was Chloe, probably feeling lonely all the time. And remember it was Chloe who made an effort to cheer me up, when she offered me her Penguin bar at break – was that because she was the only one who understood how I felt?

Dad asked me what I want for Christmas, and I told him a mobile phone, and he said, 'We'll see,' which probably means yes, so I left the brochure open on the kitchen table with a ring around the one I want. I'm sure I'm the only one in the class without one – apart from Chloe – which is truly embarrassing.

Still no sign from Mam that she's coming home. I really think she will though – I'm trying not to think about it too much, but I have a feeling she will.

The gorgeous pizza delivery boy's name is Henry, which I think is so cute. He told me we had the same taste in pizza, the last time he came round. I wonder if he noticed how fabulous I smelt. Probably not, with the pepperoni nearly knocking the two of us out.

Henry and Elizabeth – sounds like a royal couple. Wonder what his second name is. He never wears gloves, even when it's really freezing. He has a thin silver ring on his first finger, a bit like the one that Mam used to wear. And there's a tiny hole in the knee of his jeans that just makes me melt.

By the way, my nails are growing out nicely since I stopped biting them. It was pretty easy in the end. I got some pearly pink nail varnish like Miss Purtill, but I don't think it's me really. It's not loud enough, if you know what I mean. (Not that I'm loud, of course – I'm a real lady, ha ha.)

Last Saturday Ruth Wallace told me she could smell my breath a mile away, and it was like mouldy cheese. I'm getting very tired of her stupid comments. One of these days, I might just have to think up some of my own, wheelchair or no wheelchair.

 henry elizabeth

A quarter to eight, Friday, middle of December.
The show at the Comp was on last night, and it was brilliant. Chloe and I had to sit about halfway down the hall, but there was nobody tall sitting in front of us, so we could see the stage quite well.

I spent a lot of the first half looking for Bumble. He was quite hard to find, since he was just one of the gang, but I finally spotted him. He was wearing a bomber jacket and drainpipe jeans, and his hair was greased back. He looked older – and quite sexy, actually.

Wonder if anyone fancies him.

Catherine Eggleston wasn't bad as Sandy, but her singing was nothing special, except that it sure was LOUD – boy, could she belt out those songs. And she didn't forget any of her lines, which was probably a good thing.

Chris Thompson was excellent as Danny. He totally

got the American accent, and he was brilliant at singing and dancing, much better probably than poor Bumble would have been, I have to say. Oh, and Chris's voice has well and truly broken – he sounds great now.

At the interval, Chloe and I got warmish bottles of orange and chatted to a few of our old classmates who were in the audience, or helping out around the place.

And guess what – Trudy Higgins, Catherine Eggleston's best friend (the one who got the dead beetle in her lunchbox, remember?) told us that Terry McNamara, who played Kenickie, was heartbroken when Catherine Eggleston finished with him, and that it was really awkward while they were rehearsing.

Funny, I assumed it was Terry who had broken up with Catherine, not the other way around. But I suppose it makes sense really – Catherine Eggleston is just the type who'd break people's hearts.

After the show, Chloe and I were hanging around the door waiting for my dad to pick us up, and I was keeping an eye out for Bumble, when who should come over to us but Chris. He said 'hi' and the three of us chatted for a while.

He asked us how we liked our school, and he seemed really interested, you know? Not just as if he was being polite. I'd never really had a proper conversation with him before.

And wouldn't you know it, just then Dad drove up and we had to say goodbye. But as we were walking towards the car, Chris called after us to say that a gang of them were going to Nosh on the first day of the Christmas holidays for lunch, if we wanted to meet up.

Nosh is a really cool burger bar with loads of cartoon characters painted on the walls, and paper tablecloths that you're allowed to draw on with crayons.

I think we'll go. Chloe says she doesn't know if she will, but she always says that, and I always manage to persuade her.

I'd kind of like to see Chris again. And Bumble, of course – he'll probably be at Nosh too. I'm sorry I missed him after the show. Must phone him later to tell him how great it was.

chris

elizabeth

MAJORIE DINNER MAJORIE D
MAJORIE DINNER MAJORIE D
MAJORIE DINNER MAJORIE D
MAJORIE DINNER MAJORIE D
MAJORIE DINNER MAJORIE D
MAJORIE DINNER MAJORIE D
NER WITH
NER WITH
NER WITH
NER WITH
NER WITH

Five past three, Saturday, a week before Christmas.
Today is not turning out too well.

At breakfast this morning Dad asked me how I'd feel about going to Marjorie Maloney's house for Christmas dinner. I suppose I should have seen that coming really, but I didn't. It had never once occurred to me that of all the people we could spend Christmas Day with, we might end up with her.

I felt like telling him I'd rather drink sour milk out of a mucky boot, but ... well, it's kind of hard to explain, but the way he asked me, as if he really cared about what I wanted, as if he'd understand if I said I didn't fancy it ... I mean, he could have just told me we were going, couldn't he? What could I have done? Stayed at home by myself and had beans on toast?

So anyway, it felt like he was treating me like a grown-up, which made me feel that I should act like a grown-up, so I couldn't stamp my foot and throw something. I was tempted to do that a bit – and there was a jug of milk on the table that would have been perfect – but instead I managed to say, 'I suppose it's OK, if that's what you want.'

It's Christmas for him too – I had to remember that. And Marjorie *is* his friend, after all. I mean, it would be almost like me asking him if Chloe could come around here and have dinner with us. Almost, but not quite.

Anyway, I have to say it felt good when he smiled and said, 'Thanks Liz.'

And it's better that we're going over to her house, instead of the other way around, so it won't feel like she's taking Mam's place at all. And there are going to be other people there too: Marjorie's brother and his wife and their two kids, who all live in Cork, and Marjorie's father who lives with them. So there'll be quite a crowd, which actually might be a lot better than just Dad and me here, all by ourselves.

For one thing, we won't really be able to think about Mam too much, with all the other people around. And for another, you can be sure Marjorie's turkey will be a lot better than anything that Dad and I could manage.

Bet it won't be half as nice as Mam's though.

Right, I'm off now to revise for our Christmas tests. History and maths tomorrow, and I'm afraid I haven't improved much in history since the parent-teacher meeting. Today Mr O'Connor said he hoped I wasn't considering a career in anything that involved history. I promised him that it had never occurred to me.

Holidays in three more days, hurrah – and I've managed to persuade Chloe to come to Nosh. Wonder if Chris will sit beside me.

She's not coming home.

A parcel arrived from San Francisco today. Dad happened to be in the house, waiting for a chimney sweep, so he took in the parcel and left it in my room.

Here's what was inside:

1.   A red sweatshirt with a cat on the front of it
2.   A Hershey's selection box
3.   A silver bangle
4.   A Wallace & Gromit watch
5.   A letter wishing me a very Happy Christmas and saying that she was so sorry that we wouldn't be together, but that she hoped that Dad and I would have a great time, and she'd be thinking of me.

As soon as I had taken everything out of the box, I went downstairs and told Dad that I didn't want to talk to Mam when she rang.

He didn't ask me why, just nodded and said we'd take

the phone off the hook after dinner. He's great sometimes.

I'll talk to her tomorrow, but I can't today. I can't go on the phone and say thanks for the presents, when what I really want to say is how could you do this to your only child, and don't you care about me any more? And I miss you so much and I feel so sad and I haven't seen you in a whole year and you're not even coming home for Christmas. And you're a rotten mother.

I was so sure she was coming that I never sent her anything. I'll have to find something tomorrow and post it, and it'll be dead late.

And it serves her right.

Ten to nine, Wednesday before Christmas.
We got holidays today. I wish I could feel happier about that, but I'm still mad about Mam not coming home. I'm trying to be sensible and grown up about it, telling myself that she has to be home soon, that she can't stay away forever, but it's not helping much.

Chloe was really nice about it. She said it must be awful for me, and she invited me around to her house the day after Christmas, when they always have curry. I told her I'd love to. I don't think curries have too much garlic in them.

We went to meet the others for lunch at Nosh today, even though I didn't really feel like it, because I thought it might cheer me up to meet Chris and Bumble. Little did I know.

Chloe and I were the first to arrive, so we sat at a table and I picked up a crayon and drew a picture of Bart Simpson that Chloe said was exactly like him. She tried to draw Sylvester, the cat who chases Tweetie Bird, but I have to say it could have been any cat.

After about ten minutes the others started coming in, and soon there were nearly ten of us, including Terry McNamara, who didn't look as if he was missing Catherine Eggleston at all. In fact, I think he's already forgotten about her, because a few of the others were slagging him about some other girl, someone Chloe and I didn't know, and he was blushing and pretending not to know what they were on about.

Some boys are so fickle.

I was beginning to wonder if Chris was ever going to show up, when in walked Bumble. And you'll never in a million years guess who walked in with him.

Well, maybe you will. Maybe I'm the only one who didn't see it coming. It was Catherine Eggleston, and they were holding hands. And Bumble was smiling as if he'd just won the lotto.

Well, I can tell you it nearly knocked my socks off when I saw them together. Bumble and I used to laugh about Catherine Eggleston all the time in primary school – how daft she was, with her fancy schoolbags and her silly giggles. How she always sucked up to Santa, answering questions in a little girl voice that made me want to throw something at her.

We used to wonder what Terry could possibly see in her.

And now here was Bumble, obviously going out with her, holding hands with her, sitting beside her and looking at her as if she was Cleopatra, and barely saying hello to his oldest friend. (That's me, in case you're wondering.)

I hardly noticed when Chris Thompson arrived and pulled a chair in between Chloe and me. I had to drag my eyes away from the other two when Chris started talking to me. And in case you're thinking now that I was jealous of Catherine, let me tell you here and now that whatever else I felt, it *wasn't* jealousy – no way.

I mean, going out with Bumble would be like going out with my brother.

I just couldn't believe it, that was all. Bumble and Catherine Eggleston – it was the last thing I thought I'd ever see.

Poor Bumble couldn't help it, of course – she's obviously got some kind of power over boys. It's probably connected to the blonde hair (although I can NOT understand what all the fuss is about there. I think red is a much more attractive and interesting hair colour), and I suppose the boobs must have something to do with it too (although I can't understand what *that's* all about either).

But anyone can see it's only a matter of time before Bumble's heart gets broken too, and I just can't bear the thought of that. Hopefully he'll recover as quickly as Terry did. Terry hardly looked at the two of them, and didn't seem a bit bothered.

So anyway, there we all were:

Me trying not to stare at Bumble,

Chris trying to talk to me,

Bumble trying not to drool at Catherine,

Terry trying to pretend he wasn't mad about someone else,

and Chloe trying to draw Road Runner.

It sure was a long lunch.

I wonder when they started going out, and how it happened. Had Bumble secretly fancied her for ages, even when he was still my best friend? I thought we told each other everything. I know I told *him* everything – except for the shoplifting.

I wonder what he got her for Christmas. He sent me a card with a reindeer on it. Just a card, no present. Last year we went shopping together before Christmas, and bought each other scarves. He got me a lovely lilac one – of course I picked it out – and I got him a blue and red check one that I chose too.

Luckily, I hadn't posted the DVD I'd bought for him by the time his card arrived, so it's still sitting on a chair in my room. Maybe I'll watch it some time, although ninety minutes of 'Chelsea's Greatest Goals' isn't exactly my idea of excitement.

So when lunch finished after about a hundred years, we all went our separate ways.

I bought Mam a book of dessert recipes and posted it off in a padded envelope, along with the card I wrote last night, that just said 'Happy Christmas from Liz' on the inside.

I bought Dad a bottle of aftershave. Well, he's almost out of it, and if I don't buy it for him, he'll buy it himself. He might as well smell nice for Marjorie on Christmas Day.

I'm beginning to think that Scrooge had the right idea about Christmas. I mean, what's the big deal?

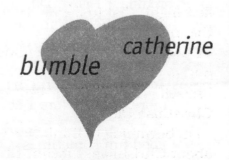

bumble catherine

Eight o'clock, Sunday, the day after Christmas.

OK, I have to say that Christmas Day in Marjorie Maloney's house went a lot better than I'd been expecting.

The day started off well. Dad and I made smoothies for breakfast, with bananas and honey and yoghurt. I added a teaspoon of Nutella to mine, which made it a weird muddy colour, but it tasted pretty good. Then after breakfast I gave Dad his aftershave and he gave me the new mobile phone I'd been begging him for forever. He said he only got it so he'd have a bit of peace. I said he'll have plenty of peace as long as he keeps me in credit, and he groaned and asked how many more years before I could leave school and get a job.

He's good fun sometimes.

I tried not to think too much about Mam not being there, and he probably did too. When she was around we always had omelettes for breakfast on Christmas morning.

I think that's why we did smoothies this time instead.

Mam phoned around two, earlier than usual, because I'd told her that Dad and I were going out for Christmas dinner. She probably thought I meant to a restaurant, and I didn't mention Marjorie. It's got nothing to do with Mam who Dad and I celebrate Christmas with any more. I listened to her wishing me Happy Christmas and telling me how much she missed me, and after a while, I told her that Dad was waiting, and hung up.

I told her about my new mobile, and she took the number. Big deal.

At about half two, Dad and I went across the road to Marjorie's, and I must say the dinner was excellent. This was the menu:

***

Turkey with absolutely no burnt bits
Roast potatoes scattered with rosemary
Carrot fingers, all buttery
Roast parsnips with a yummy parmesan coating
Little balls of really good stuffing made with chestnuts
Gravy that made me want to lick my plate at the end

For dessert, which I barely had room for, we didn't have plum pudding, which was a big relief because it's my least favourite dessert ever. We had a kind of rolled-up chocolate cake, which Marjorie said is called a roulade, filled with whipped cream and topped with some kind of roasted nuts. I'm not sure, but I think it might just be the best dessert I ever tasted.

One thing about Marjorie Maloney, she sure can cook. No wonder her bum is quite big.

Her brother Kevin was great fun, organising loads of games and stuff. And her dad was a bit drunk, I think, because he kept falling asleep in an armchair, and even during dinner he nodded off for a few minutes. Nobody noticed until all the talking stopped for a second, and then we heard him snoring. I don't know how he didn't fall off his chair – I'm sure I would have.

I must practise sleeping in a chair and not falling off. You never know when it might come in handy.

The two kids were OK too, a five-year-old girl called Sarah and a three-year-old boy called Luke. I painted Sarah's nails and dressed her up in an old evening dress and high heels that Marjorie gave us, and then Luke began to cry because he wanted to be dressed up too, so I put his grandad's hat on him, and an old green raincoat I found in Marjorie's utility room.

Their mother said I'd make a good big sister, and for some reason Marjorie went scarlet.

I found out a lot about Marjorie over dinner, actually. It turns out she was an au pair in France for two years, and now she works from home as a translator. She speaks Spanish too, but she likes French better. I almost told her that French is one of my worst subjects in school, next to history, but I stopped myself just in time. She might have offered to give me a grind, which of course Dad would have jumped at.

But even though she's a lot nicer than I thought, I still don't want Dad to get too friendly with her. We don't need anyone getting too close – we're managing fine on our own, Dad and me.

Anyway, we stayed until about nine o'clock, when Luke and Sarah were put to bed in Marjorie's smallest bedroom. Then Dad and I walked back across the road, and when we got inside, Dad said, 'Will we sit in the garden for a little while?'

We used to do that all the time when I was small, me and Mam and Dad, just wrap ourselves up in rugs or blankets and sit outside at night, after the dinner stuff was cleared away. I'd be tucked in between them, leaning against Dad's shoulder or pressed up to Mam's arm, sniffing her almondy smell.

They'd usually do most of the talking, grown-up stuff that would float away into the dark, and sometimes one of them would laugh, and I'd tilt my head up and try to count the stars, and it would feel so safe and cosy.

I can't remember when we stopped doing that.

The weather was nice last night – cold, but very starry and still. So we took two blankets out of the airing cupboard and we went to sit out on the garden seat to look at the stars, which were all out by then.

We could see our breath in front of us. It looked like we were smoking. I thought about saying that to Dad, but then decided not to. (And just in case you're wondering, I only had a few puffs once, and it made me feel like throwing up – yeuk. Smoking's for idiots.)

So there the two of us were, wrapped in our blankets looking up at the zillions of stars, and remembering when it used to be three of us. At least, I was remembering, and Dad probably was too.

And because it was dark all around, I asked Dad if he

missed Mam at all. I didn't look at his face, just up at the sky. And I had time to count seven stars before he said yes, sometimes.

And then, maybe because it was dark all around, Dad asked me if I was OK about it being just the two of us now, and it took me a lot longer than seven stars before I said that sometimes I was still lonely, but mostly I was OK.

It was sad, on the garden seat. I told him about Bumble and Catherine, and he teased me about always wanting to be the one to open the door when Henry the pizza delivery boy came, and I said that we must try and make Marjorie's chestnut stuffing some time, and we found the Plough and the North Star in the sky.

But it was still sad.

After a while we went in, and I said goodnight to Dad. And as I was undressing, my new phone started to beep, and I opened my very first text message, which was from San Francisco and which said:

Happy Christmas my darling girl xxx.

I didn't answer it.

Now it's the day after Christmas, and I've just got back from Chloe's house. Her Dad made the curry, and they had all the proper Indian stuff like poppadums and naan and everything. Her little brother was a bit of a nuisance, though. He's seven, and a real baby. He kept banging on Chloe's bedroom door when we were trying to listen to her new Norah Jones CD after dinner.

Maybe it's just as well I don't have a little brother or sister.

TERRIBLE

Five past ten, Friday, 31st December, the worst day in the world. I did a terrible thing today.

You remember Ruth Wallace, my neighbour in the wheelchair? You know how nasty she is to me, and how I try to ignore her when she says or does all those mean things?

Well, today I failed. Today I finally lost my temper with her, and I think I may be in very big trouble now, even bigger than the shoplifting.

Here's what happened. When I got up this morning, I discovered we were out of milk, so I shouted up to Dad that I was going to the shop, which is just two blocks away. As soon as I came out I saw her, just sitting by her gate, all muffled up because it was pretty cold, with a furry black hat on her head and a brown and orange check blanket over her legs.

When she saw me coming she actually smiled, and I automatically smiled back – well, half-smiled. I didn't feel like giving her a proper smile.

As I walked past, she stuck out her hand and grabbed my wrist, and boy, were her fingers freezing – like ice. I opened my mouth to tell her to let me go, but before I had a chance, she said, kind of softly, 'I'm just wondering what it feels like.'

I thought she meant my hand. I tried to pull away, but she held on tight. And do you know what she said then?

She said, 'What does it feel like when your mother leaves you?'

And the awful thing is that she was smiling all the time, this horrible fake smile, and she had a bit of a Cornflake or something caught between her teeth, and I pulled my arm away and walked as quickly as I could down the road, and I could hear her laughing, and then these tears just came out of nowhere, and I had to keep wiping them away, because I couldn't see where I was going.

And all the way to the shop, I could feel the tingle that I always feel when my temper is just about ready to be lost. I kept hearing her laughing, sitting there in her horrible wheelchair and laughing at me. I bought the milk, in one of those plastic litre containers with a handle, and a pack of tissues so I could dry my face up. No way was I going to let her see that she'd made me cry.

She was still there when I got back, still sitting there, grinning away. I walked towards her, trying to ignore her, trying to keep my temper under control. And if she'd said nothing, I don't think I would have done anything, I really don't – except maybe given her a filthy look.

If only she'd kept quiet.

But she didn't. She watched me as I walked towards her, and then she said, in this horrible pretending-to-care voice, 'Hey Liz, have you been crying?'

And that did it. Something came racing up inside me like a tidal wave. I lifted the plastic container of milk and I rammed it down onto her legs as hard as I could, and then I turned and ran. I bolted in our gate and up the path and around to the back of the house, right down to the bottom of the garden.

My heart was thumping really loudly, and my hands were shaking – I had to wrap them right around the milk to keep from dropping it. It was a cold morning, I could see my breath coming out in fast little puffs, but I didn't dare go into the house. I was afraid Ruth Wallace's parents would come banging at the door, looking for me.

After a while I had to move, I was so cold. I walked up the garden on legs I could hardly feel and opened the back door, sure that Mrs Wallace would be inside, waiting for me. But there was nobody there except Dad, wondering why I'd taken so long. No sign of the Wallaces at all.

All through breakfast, which I had to force myself to eat, I kept waiting to hear the doorbell. When it finally rang, I almost fell out of my chair, but it was just the boy who delivered our paper, looking for his money. While Dad was talking to him, I crept into the sitting room and peeped through the window.

Nobody in next door's garden, no sign of anyone. No shouts of anger coming from the house. Nobody storming out and turning in our gate with a face like thunder. I couldn't understand it.

And now it's almost bedtime, and I haven't dared to put my nose outside the door all day. Chloe came around after lunch and we watched a film with Colin Farrell in it, and I haven't a clue what it was about, because all I could see was my arm lifting up the milk and bringing it down with a thump on Ruth Wallace's useless legs.

I wish I could start today all over again. I wish I could rub it out and begin again.

I wish Mam was here now. I know I was mad at her for not coming home, but it's only because I miss her so much. Sometimes it feels like a real pain, right in the middle of me, where I think my heart must be. Other times it's like I'm empty, as if someone came along and held me upside down for a while and let everything fall out.

That's how it feels when your mother leaves, Ruth Wallace.

I wish this was all a crazy kind of dream, and I could wake up and Mam would be there with my breakfast on a tray, like she used to do some weekend mornings, with a soft boiled egg and brown toast soldiers, or a bowl of lump-free porridge topped with a blob of blackcurrant jam. I wish I had magical powers like Harry Potter, and I could wave my wand and change everything back to how it used to be.

I wrote this text to Mam a while ago:

Hit Ruth Wallace on legs with milk. Please help.
— but then I got scared, and deleted it. I can't tell Mam what I did. I can't tell anyone.

I hope to God Ruth Wallace is OK.

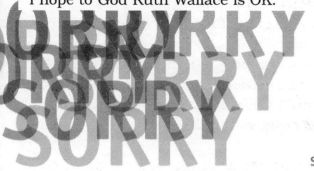

SORRY

WEIRD.

Just before dinner, Tuesday, 4th January.
This is weird. It's been four days since I attacked Ruth Wallace, and absolutely nothing has happened. What is going on? Why has nobody come around to demand an explanation?

And why haven't I seen any sign of Ruth in the last four days? Where is she?

I can only think of two possible explanations. One is that she's dead, or at least so badly injured that she can't tell anyone who did it. I try not to think about that one.

The other is that she's OK, and she just didn't tell anyone what I did – but that doesn't make sense. Surely Ruth Wallace would be delighted to have an excuse to get me into trouble – and surely I gave her the perfect excuse, didn't I? I assaulted her. I attacked a helpless invalid with a full litre of milk.

Like I said, it's weird.

Maybe she's doing this on purpose – staying out of the way just to scare me. Well if she is, her plan is working brilliantly. I can't sleep at night, thinking about what might be happening next door.

And I can hardly eat – well, just bits of things. Yesterday I had half a Weetabix, two mandarin oranges, three fish fingers, a few spoonfuls of Ben & Jerry's and a bowl of popcorn. (Well, I was starving by bedtime, so I had to come up with something quick, and it was the popcorn you do in the microwave.)

Dad keeps asking me if I'm OK. Imagine what he'd say if I told him what I'd done.

Mam spent Christmas with Enda and George in a log cabin that George's family owns in some mountains. She says it was raining most of the time, but they went walking a lot. She's back at work now. So is Dad, so I have the house to myself every day until next Monday, when I go back to school.

Chloe is in Kerry till the weekend.

I haven't seen Bumble since the lunch in Nosh. I wonder how his big romance is getting on. I wish we were still best friends, and I could tell him about Ruth. He's probably the only person in the world who wouldn't be shocked and horrified.

So what else is new? I've been sending a few texts, trying to get used to it, but I'm still really slow. I think you're supposed to leave out most of the vowels, so I sent this one to Dad a few days ago:

`Jst prctsng`

And he texted me back with this:

`Next time try English.`

Yesterday I sent Mam this one:

```
Hpy Nw Yr frm Lz.
```

I suppose it did look a bit like Chinese, but Mam understood it. This was her answer:

```
Same 2 u xxx
```

It's no use – I can't think about anything else except Ruth Wallace. Hang on – Dad just called upstairs that I'm wanted on the phone. It can't be Mam – it's too early for her.

Later

You won't believe who it was – Chris Thompson.

He wants to meet me. I'm in shock. He got my number from Bumble. Did you get that? He asked Bumble for my number.

My hands are shaking. I can hardly write. My heart is hammering. I hope my voice didn't wobble when I was talking to him. I can hardly remember what we talked about.

We're going to the cinema, on Friday night – God, that's only three days away. He told me what's on, but I can't remember. I won't be able to concentrate on a minute of it anyway, with him sitting beside me.

Oh my God – what if he puts his arm around me? What if anyone sees us? Am I supposed to slap his face if he tries anything, or what?

OK Liz, get a grip. It's only a date.

Oh my God – a DATE. My first ever date – and with a really cute guy too. Did I mention his gorgeous dimple? And how amazing he was in *Grease*?

I feel faint. Maybe I'd better eat something.

I couldn't eat more than two bites of Dad's macaroni cheese. He felt my forehead and asked me if I was OK. I told him it was my time of month, which shut him right up.

Between Ruth Wallace and Chris Thompson, I'm probably going to fade away from starvation, or collapse from lack of sleep.

God, I've just thought of something else. Do I pay for myself at the cinema, or does he? Or do I sort of pretend to want to pay, and is he supposed to jump in and insist on doing it? How does anyone know what to do in these situations? Who makes up the rules, and where can I read them?

I want Mam. She phoned while Dad and I were washing up, but I couldn't tell her – I just couldn't say it on the phone. I wanted to sit beside her and look at her face, and ask her a million questions. And of course I couldn't tell her about attacking Ruth Wallace either – another thing I had to keep from her.

And I can't call Chloe to ask about Chris, because I don't know the number in Kerry, and Chloe is the only other person in Ireland without a mobile phone. Bugger. Not that Chloe would be any help really though – she's never had a date either – but at least I could talk to her about it.

Catherine Eggleston would be able to give me loads of tips, but I'd rather eat maggots on toast than ask her.

And oh God, what do I do if Chris tries to kiss me? I have no idea how to kiss anyone, apart from my parents and Granny Daly, and something tells me this is going to be very different. Now I really feel sick. Maybe I'll ring him and tell him I have an infectious disease and I've been forbidden to go outside for at least three years.

But then I'd just have to go through all this again the next time somebody asked me out – that's if anyone else ever does – so maybe I should just get it over with now.

I haven't told Dad yet. Obviously he knows about Chris calling, because he answered the phone. Although he didn't ask me who it was afterwards, which I thought was very nice of him – he was probably dying to know. Or maybe he just assumed it was Bumble.

I'll tell him I'm meeting a school friend at the cinema, which is true, sort of. He might be going out himself on Friday night with Marjorie – oh God, what if they go to the cinema too? Imagine if we all met up in the foyer. I think I'd die.

It's past midnight. I'd better go to bed, although I know I won't sleep. My head is bursting with worry and excitement.

Can you believe I actually forgot about Ruth Wallace for a while there? I've just remembered her again now.

I don't know what's more terrifying, being arrested for murdering your neighbour or going on your first date.

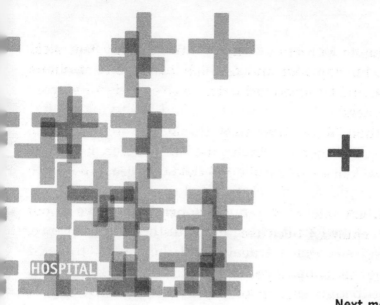

HOSPITAL

Next morning.

She's in hospital.

Ruth Wallace is in hospital, and I'm to blame.

Dad told me at breakfast, just a while ago. (Of course I was up in time to have breakfast with him before he went off to work – I didn't fall asleep till around two, and I woke before seven.) I got such a shock when he said it, I almost choked on my Weetabix. He had to thump me on the back.

When I could talk again, I asked him what was wrong with Ruth, hoping he'd say a chest infection, or a fractured skull, or something, but he said, 'She's having some kind of operation on her legs, I think,' and I had to drop my spoon on the floor so I could disappear under the table for a minute.

It's *definitely* my fault. It has to be.

When I came back up, I asked Dad if he knew what hospital Ruth was in, and he said no, and then he gave me a funny look, so I stopped talking about Ruth and tried to finish my Weetabix, which tasted even more like straw than it usually does.

And now Dad's gone to work, and I'm trying to find the courage to do what I have to do.

I have to find out which hospital she's in. I have to ring the bell at the Wallaces' house and ask whoever comes to the door which hospital Ruth is in.

And then I have to go and see her, and I have to tell her I'm sorry for attacking her with the milk. If I don't, I'll never sleep or eat again, and they're two things I really enjoy doing.

Right, better get it over with. Wish me luck. If this diary stops suddenly, you'll know it's because I'm in prison.

Later

Thank goodness Ruth's nice brother Damien answered the door. I was really hoping he would.

He smiled and said, 'Hello Liz,' when he saw me, and didn't try to slam the door in my face, which I was half expecting. (So it does look like Ruth hasn't told anyone what I did, which I still can't understand, but which I'm not going to worry about right now.)

I told Damien that I'd heard Ruth was in hospital, and that I'd like to go and see her. I still felt a bit scared that he was going to tell me to get lost, since I was the one who'd put her there, but he didn't. He said, 'Hey, that's really nice of you,' which of course made me feel ten times guiltier, and then he told me which hospital she was in.

It wasn't until I got back here that I realised I never asked him how she was.

I'll go to see her tomorrow, which is Thursday, because this is one of those things that will only get harder the longer I put it off – and because I don't want it hanging over me when I meet Chris on Friday.

The only good thing about being so worried about Ruth is that I haven't time to worry about Chris.

I'll take some apples with me – I'll pick the least wrinkly ones out of the fruit bowl. I'll tell her that I'm sorry.

Even writing it down makes me want to get sick. The thought of walking into her room, or ward, or wherever she is, makes my stomach do a flip-flop. But I have to.

What'll she say? I have no idea. Maybe she'll start shouting at me to go away and leave her alone, and a nurse will come running over to see what all the noise is about, and Ruth will tell her what I did, and the nurse will look at me as if I'm a criminal and make me leave the hospital, probably march me off with a hand on my arm, like the store detective in Boots, and everyone will be looking at me.

Or maybe Ruth will be too weak to say anything. Maybe she'll just give me a filthy look with her dying eyes. I think that would probably be worse.

I wish I could talk to someone about this, but who? Not Dad, definitely. I absolutely can't tell him – he'd hit the roof. And not Chloe – I'm not sure that she'd understand.

Bumble would understand, but he'd probably tell Catherine Eggleston, and she's the last person I'd want to know.

I'd tell Mam, if she was here face to face. But not on the phone. I can't say it on the phone, I can't text it, I can't email it. If *only* she was here.

Have I mentioned how much I miss her?

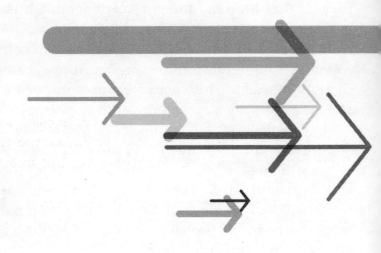

Ten to eight, next day.

Well, I did it – it's over. It was probably the hardest thing I ever had to do in my life so far, but at least it's over now.

Here's what happened. I set off after lunch – I mean after the half banana that was all I could eat. (I wonder how much weight I've lost over the past week?)

It took me just under an hour to walk to the hospital. I could have got a bus, but it was quite a nice day – and I wasn't exactly in a hurry to arrive.

It was a quarter to three by the time I got there. I hadn't even thought about visiting hours, but there was a big notice just inside the main door saying they were between one thirty and three o'clock, so that was OK.

I figured a quarter of an hour would be more than enough. Two minutes would have been more than enough.

The hospital smelt like bleach and rashers. I tried to make myself look as old as possible, in case they had a rule about not allowing children in, but the woman behind the desk didn't seem too bothered about my age, just told me where to go when I said I'd come to see Ruth Wallace.

I wondered if Ruth had a room to herself, but I was too nervous to ask.

I had to go up two flights of stairs. I could have taken the lift, but lifts make me want to throw up, and since I already felt a bit like that I thought I'd better stick to the stairs. There were loads of people walking about, some just in dressing gowns and slippers.

I didn't see anyone in a wheelchair.

Halfway up the second flight of stairs, I suddenly remembered that I'd forgotten to bring the apples from the fruit bowl. I thought about going back down to the hospital shop and getting something there, but when I checked my pockets I only had sixty-seven cents, and I was pretty sure I wouldn't get anything for that.

Anyway, maybe when you were visiting someone to apologise for assaulting them, you weren't supposed to bring them a present. Maybe that was what Granny Daly would call *ADDING INSULT TO INJURY.*

When I got to the second floor I looked for room 23A. My tummy was flip-flopping like anything, and my legs felt pretty wobbly. I tried taking a few deep breaths, but that just made me feel like I was eating bleach-flavoured rashers.

The door of 23A was closed, so I gave a little knock and waited. I didn't hear anything, even when I pressed my ear up to it, but there was a lot of noise in the corridor, trolleys wheeling and people talking and cups clinking. In the end, I just opened the door a bit and peeped in.

First I thought I must have got the wrong room, because there was a girl I didn't recognise in the bed. She was facing the door and she looked very pale, and when she saw me she closed her eyes. I was just about to say 'sorry' and back out when I saw the end of a second bed poking out from behind a curtain, and my heart began to thump all over again.

I walked over to the curtain and peeped around.

Ruth Wallace looked at me and I looked at her, and for what seemed like ages none of us said anything. I was too busy trying to find the right words, and she was probably too gobsmacked.

At least she didn't look like she was dying. She was a bit pale, but not ghostly white. She did look small though, smaller than when she sat in her wheelchair, and not half as tough. I think it was the first time I had seen her without a hat on. I could see the pink of her head under her hair.

There was something big under the bedclothes around where her legs were, like a frame or something – probably to keep people like me from whacking them again.

At last I opened my mouth and 'I came to see you' was what fell out. Which I know was pretty idiotic, but it was all I could think of.

Ruth Wallace blinked once, and that was all she did. Her face was blank – she didn't look cross, or sad, or anything. Just small and thin, with that big boxy shape around her legs.

There was a tube of something going into the back of one of her hands, and a white plastic-looking strip around the same wrist, like a skinny bracelet, with something written on it that I couldn't read.

Then I said, 'I'm sorry I hit you with the milk.' Quietly, so the girl in the next bed wouldn't hear me.

And all the time, my heart was pumping away in my chest, and my tummy was doing somersaults. And then, because Ruth was still just looking blankly at me, I said the next thing that popped into my head, which was 'I forgot to bring you anything'.

Still no answer. I was beginning to feel a bit desperate – was she just going to keep staring at me until I left? Maybe if I asked her a question she'd have to answer, so I said, 'How are you feeling?'

First I thought she wasn't going to say anything. She blinked two more times, and then she put up a hand – the one without the tube attached – and rubbed at her nose, and then she turned her head away from me so it was facing the wall.

I snuck a glance at her locker and saw a box of Maltesers and a bundle of Tracy Beaker magazines and a furry white toy cat all sitting on top.

And then, all of a sudden, she turned back to me and said, 'It wasn't because of that.'

I said, 'What?' because I wasn't sure what she meant.

'It wasn't because you hit me. You hit like a girl. I was going to have the operation anyway.'

And then, before I had a chance to say anything, do

you know what she said? She said, 'I probably deserved it anyway.' She kept her eyes on my face all the time and she didn't blink, not once.

And all I could think of to say to that was, 'Oh.' It was a lot to take in:

It wasn't my fault that she was in hospital.

I wasn't even strong enough to hurt a helpless invalid.

She didn't really blame me for hitting her.

And then I realised something else: she didn't have to tell me that it wasn't my fault. She could have said nothing, and let me go on thinking that I was to blame, but she didn't.

Which was the first nice thing Ruth Wallace had ever done for me.

And saying that she deserved it – well, that was almost the same as telling me she was sorry, which was the *last* thing I had been expecting. *I* was the one who was supposed to be saying sorry here.

Just then, a bell rang in the corridor, and she said, 'You have to go now.' And then she closed her eyes, and I waited a minute to see if she'd open them again, but she didn't, so I turned around and walked out. The girl in the other bed still had her eyes closed, but she probably heard every word.

And all the way downstairs, I was still trying to get my head around the fact that I had just had my first ever conversation with Ruth Wallace. And nobody had shouted, and nobody had said anything nasty.

And all the way home, I thought about how I'd been worrying myself sick for the past few days, how I'd tossed and turned in bed every night, waiting for someone to find out what a terrible thing I'd done, wondering if Ruth Wallace was dead, or seriously injured.

Imagine she reads Tracey Beaker, just like me. I wonder what music she listens to – wouldn't it be funny if she liked Eminem?

Hit like a girl, indeed. I'd like to see *her* try and hurt someone with a litre of milk.

But thank goodness that's all over, and I can concentrate on the next terrifying thing in my life – my first ever date, tomorrow night.

I think I'm going to throw up.

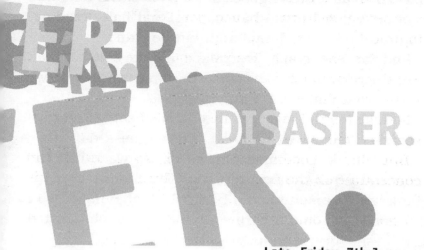

Talk about a disaster.

It started off OK. Chris was waiting for me at the corner of the cinema block, which was just as well, because I was ready to run home again if he wasn't.

He smelt nice, but he looked a bit strange. His clothes were fine – he wore black jeans and a grey shirt, and a leather jacket that looked new – but he had stuff in his hair, some kind of gel, or something, that made it all stick up as if someone had just given him a fright. It was a real pity, because Chris has lovely floppy hair. He probably thought it made him look cool.

Anyway, I began to relax a bit when I saw him, especially when he smiled. He really has the most gorgeous smile. His dimple is so much cuter than mine, it's not fair.

As we walked towards the cinema, Chris began telling me about the digital camera he'd got for Christmas, but

I wasn't really listening, because all I kept thinking was 'I'm on a date.' I was half hoping, and half dreading, that he'd try to hold my hand, but he didn't.

And then, as soon as we walked into the cinema, it all went horribly wrong, because the first two people we saw were Bumble and Catherine.

It was AWFUL. We had to talk to them, of course, because they saw us too. And – you've guessed it – they were going to the same film as us, so we joined the queue together as if we were four best friends.

For some reason I could hardly look at Bumble, so I concentrated on Catherine, trying to look interested while she bragged about the clothes she'd got for Christmas, and the gold watch her godmother or someone had given her, and the skiing trip she's going on at mid-term. I was bored after the first three words.

And naturally, we all had to sit together inside. I couldn't really see Bumble and Catherine, because they were on the other side of Chris, but I sure found it hard to concentrate on the film. If you asked me what it was about, all I'd be able to tell you was that Scarlett Johannsen was in it, dressed like someone from long ago, with a bonnet and stuff, and in the end she died. I think she died anyway – I remember her in a bed looking weak, and crying a lot. (Of course, her make-up stayed perfect.)

I kept waiting for Chris to put his arm around me – I had decided not to slap his face if he did – but he didn't even try. Maybe the other two put him off. Or maybe that just never happens on first dates.

I can't believe how little I know about this kind of

stuff. They should teach it at school: the dos and don'ts of first dates. It would be a lot more useful than knowing the capital of the Czech Republic – and you can bet everyone would pay attention.

Anyway, I couldn't wait to get away from the others afterwards, so the minute we were outside I said I had a headache, and my best friend Catherine tried not to look too happy at the thought of having Bumble all to herself for the rest of the evening.

He barely looked at me when Chris and I were leaving – maybe he was glad to be rid of me too.

Chris walked me home, and he did most of the talking. I tried to be cheerful, really I did, but I wasn't very good at it. I was in a lousy mood – trust Catherine Eggleston to ruin my first ever date – and all I could manage was 'Oh yeah', and 'Really?' and stuff like that.

When we got to my house I just turned to Chris and said, 'Well thanks a lot, see you,' and bolted up the path.

So much for worrying about my first kiss.

Thank goodness Dad was still out. I left him a note telling him I'd gone to bed and went straight upstairs. I won't get up tomorrow until he's left for work, just in case he starts asking me all about tonight.

So that's the end of my first and only date with Chris. Let's hope the next time someone asks me out, Catherine Eggleston is a million miles away – preferably rolling down some ski slope and breaking at least one leg.

Chloe gets back from Kerry tomorrow, thank goodness. At least I'll have one friend to talk to, since my old one doesn't seem to want me any more, and my almost-boyfriend is history.

Back to school on Monday, as if things weren't bad enough. Actually, I don't really mind going back – at least I won't be hanging around here thinking about what a mess I make of everything. And I'm starting advanced swimming lessons after school, which I'm looking forward to.

We went swimming once a week in primary school, and I was in the advanced group in sixth class, but this is much more grown up, with all the different strokes, and races and everything. And we'll be doing life-saving too, which should be really cool.

OK, I just heard Dad coming in, so I'm off to bed in case he looks in.

ok. C U then.

hi fncy pzza 2moro nite?meet 7pm same plc?....................

Five past eight, Thursday, 13th January.
Can you believe it? Chris texted me a while ago.

I was in shock when I got his message. After the way the date turned out, I was sure he'd never want to have anything more to do with me. And then, just as I was starting my homework, this text arrived:

`Hi fncy pzza 2moro nite? Meet 7pm same plc?`

Imagine – he actually wants to see me again. I waited fifteen minutes, just so it wouldn't look like he was the only boy who wanted to go out with me, and then I texted him back:

`OK C U then`

So we're going out for a pizza tomorrow night. I'm just beginning to have that sick feeling again. I thought it was only first dates that were terrifying, but it looks like I was wrong. Maybe it takes three or four of them before you stop wanting to throw up at the thought.

I'm wondering whether to tell Dad. Will he be cross if

he finds out that I'm going on dates without saying anything? Do fathers need to know about these kinds of things? Would he be horrified at the thought of his little girl having a boyfriend?

Yes, probably. Maybe I'll say nothing just yet.

Oh and guess what else? Ruth Wallace came home from hospital yesterday, nearly a week after I went to see her. I happened to be passing the landing window as her Dad was taking the wheelchair out of the boot of his car, and I watched him opening the passenger door and lifting her out and putting her into the wheelchair very carefully, as if she was a china doll.

She had a red coat on, and nice black boots, and one of her dorky hats.

I'm not sure if she saw me. She looked towards our house for a second, and she seemed to be staring straight at the landing window, but she didn't wave or anything, and neither did I.

I wonder if she'll say anything about the magazines that appeared in her porch later on. I wonder if she'll guess who left them there.

I've started the advanced swimming after school, and it's great, much more interesting than the swimming we did in primary. Our coach is called Sandra and she gives everyone really individual attention, because there are only five of us in the class. She told us we'll be having an exhibition before Easter for our parents, and I tried not to think about Mam not being there.

One more thing she's missing out on.

Oh, and the big news from school is that our whole class is getting penfriends from France. Mr Geraghty, our French teacher, has a friend teaching in Paris who's going to get her class to write to us. We could get a boy or a girl, since the French class is mixed – we'll have to wait and see when they write back.

Chloe and I have agreed that if either of us gets a boy we'll both write to him, and hopefully he won't mind being shared.

We have to write to them in French and they'll write back to us in English, which could make things a bit tricky. I think I've already mentioned how awful my French is. Hopefully my penfriend's English will be just as bad, and we'll be quits.

And remember Henry, the gorgeous pizza delivery guy? Well, I asked him what his second name was, and it's Morrissey, which is a bit of a disappointment. I had thought of much better ones for him, like D'Arcy or Montague or Fitzwilliam. Not that it matters really – as Granny Daly would say, *WHAT'S IN A NAME?*

Someone must have given him gloves for Christmas. They're black leather ones, so they go with his jacket. And he wears a hat these days too, a woolly green one with two blue stripes at the bottom, which I have to say looks a tiny bit girly to me, but I suppose it keeps him warm. He's still the sexiest-looking boy I know. Chris is cute more than sexy.

Imagine if *Henry* phoned and asked me out – now *that* would be truly terrifying. I suppose I'd have to choose between him and Chris. Or we could meet in secret, to make it even more romantic. And then if Chris found out, they'd probably have to fight over me. Henry would probably win, because he's older and taller. I just hope he wouldn't hurt Chris too much.

There's been no sign of Bumble and Catherine around town. I suppose they're still madly in love. I wonder if Bumble will ring me when she breaks his heart. Of course, I'll be there for him, even if he has rejected my friendship, and I'll never, ever say he should have seen it coming.

Maybe Chris and I could find him someone nice, to help him forget about Catherine. Chloe would be ideal if she'd only give up the garlic.

She's coming over soon to help me decide what I'm going to wear 2moro nite, so I'd better stop. Wish me luck.

Liz ♥ Chris

PEPPORINI & ONION & PINEAPPLE & MUSHR

Well that was a big improvement, apart from the last bit.

We met at seven – actually ten past, because I dribbled toothpaste on my pink top and I had to change, but I think the girl being late is allowed. Chris was waiting for me at the same corner as before. (Maybe that'll be our corner from now on. Maybe in fifty years' time we'll be showing our grandchildren where we used to meet for our dates.)

He had the gel in his hair again, which was a bit disappointing. But he looked glad to see me, and I was still happy that he hadn't been put off me forever, so I decided I wouldn't let it bother me.

We walked to the pizza place, and thank goodness there was no sign of you-know-who there. (I mean Catherine and Bumble, in case you don't know who.) I ordered a small cheese and pineapple pizza because I didn't want Chris to think I was a savage – and also because I wasn't sure how much of it I'd manage to eat anyway, with my nerves. He didn't seem nervous at all – he ordered a medium pizza with pepperoni and onions for himself, so there wasn't much wrong with his appetite. Maybe boys don't get nervous about dating.

Anyway, it was fine – the date, I mean, not the pizza – although that was OK too. Not quite as good as the ones from Pizza Palace that Henry delivers, but good enough. Chris and I chatted away about school and stuff, and there weren't too many embarrassing silences, and I actually managed to finish most of my pizza.

So everything was going fine until we began to walk home. Chris took my hand when we got outside the restaurant, which made me flutter a bit all over again, but it was kind of nice. And everything was going very well until we got to my gate.

And then I turned to him to say goodnight, and he lunged towards me and – how can I describe it? His face bashed into mine, and his nose jammed into my cheek, and he pressed his mouth up against mine for a second, and I could smell onions, and then it was over.

My first kiss – the thing I'd been half dreading and half hoping for since I was about eight. It took about three seconds, and all I remember is his nose shoved into my cheek and the smell of onions. I was so disappointed, I could barely say goodnight to him.

Aren't kisses supposed to be wonderful, like in the films? Did I do something wrong? Or did I not do something I should have done?

Maybe we just need some practice. I'm sure it should be slower. They're always much slower, in the films. And the boy should take the girl's face in his hands, very gently, and sort of lean towards her, with a soppy look on his face. Chris did none of that. He mustn't be watching the right kind of films.

I just know Chloe is going to call me tomorrow and ask me about kissing, since we figured it was going to happen tonight. I suppose I'll have to pretend it was wonderful, so she won't be disappointed.

Like I was.

ROUND 21
LIZ v RUTH

Middle of the afternoon, Saturday, 15th January.

A funny thing happened just now.

I met Ruth Wallace. I was walking past her gate on my way home from Chloe's house, and she was wheeling herself down the path, and she had a red and blue hat on that her granny must have crocheted for her, and it was truly disgusting.

And she looked at me and nodded. And I looked at her and nodded back. And then, because she didn't look like she was going to say or do anything else, I kind of smiled.

And she kind of smiled back. And then she said, 'Your jacket is the colour of vomit.'

And quick as a flash, I said, 'At least I'm not wearing a tea cosy on my head.' It was the first time I'd ever said anything back to her.

She looked at me for a minute, and then she said, 'That skirt must have been going cheap.'

And I said, 'At least my granny didn't knit it for me.'

It was fun, in a weird kind of a way. Not nasty at all, more like a game between us. And then she turned and wheeled herself back up the path, and I came in home.

She didn't mention the magazines I left in her porch, and neither did I.

The colour of vomit, indeed. Shows how much she knows about khaki.

Later

Mam just phoned, and we chatted for a bit, and just before she hung up, she said, 'By the way, will you be at home tomorrow around two?'

And I said I would, and she said, 'Good, because I've got a surprise for you.'

And I said, 'What is it?' which I know is a really dumb question, right after someone has told you it's a surprise.

But all she'd say was, 'Wait till tomorrow, and you'll find out.' She wouldn't tell me anything else, even though I did my best nagging, which usually works on Dad.

I have no idea what it could be. It can't be something coming in the post, because tomorrow is Sunday. I'll just have to wait and see.

I love surprises.

Five to eleven, Sunday night, 16th January.
I'm all cried out. I think the last time I cried like this was the day Mam left – or maybe on my birthday, when I opened her presents. And today she made me cry again.

Dad and I had sausage and mash for lunch, which we often do on Sunday. I must say mash is one of the few things that Dad gets exactly right, all buttery and fluffy. And I always cook the sausages now, and make sure they're the same colour all over.

And all the way through lunch, I kept checking the clock on the wall, waiting for two o' clock to come. I didn't say anything to Dad about it, because we still don't really mention Mam that much.

Anyway, we were just finished, and I was thinking about whether to have ice cream for dessert, or a slice of the lemon cake that Marjorie sent over the other day. I had just decided that I'd better have a bit of both when the doorbell rang.

Straightaway, I knew it had to be the surprise. I jumped up and ran to the front door, and flung it open.

And then I nearly fainted.

I actually had to grab on to the side of the door, because I thought I was going to slide down to the floor if I didn't. I could feel my face getting cold.

And Mam said, 'Hi Liz,' and smiled a bit nervously at me.

She looked pretty much the same as I remembered. Her hair was a bit longer, but still the same colour red. She hadn't any new holes in her ears, but she was wearing a chunky orange cardigan I'd never seen, and grey jeans, and a silver bracelet that jangled when she lifted her arm to tuck her hair behind her ear.

And suddenly I really, really wanted Dad to be there.

And then finally, after about a million years, Mam stepped towards me, and at the same minute I moved towards her, and we met somewhere in the middle, and she still smelt the same, and I'm pretty sure she started crying a second before I did.

And she was saying something about missing me, and telling me she was sorry, so sorry, and I was saying nothing, just hanging on to her as if I'd never let her go.

And some time during the past year I'd managed to grow as tall as her. And I just kept hanging on and hanging on.

And when we managed to stop crying at last, when she was dabbing at my eyes with a tissue and telling me how pretty and grown-up I'd got, Dad appeared. He was quiet, but very polite. He invited Mam in, and we all sat down at the kitchen table, and Mam gave me a pink South Park t-shirt and a new box of watercolour paints.

She didn't bring anything for Dad, which wasn't surprising, but still a bit embarrassing. He didn't seem to mind though. He made coffee, and Mam looked surprised when he gave me a cup, but she didn't say anything.

After a bit of talking about nothing – the flight home, Granny Daly, the weather in San Francisco – Mam asked if I wanted to go for a walk. I looked at Dad, because it all felt a bit weird, but he just nodded and said he'd wash up and see me later.

Outside the house I looked for Mam's red Clio, but the only car around was a green Micra. Mam told me she'd sold the Clio before she went away, and the Micra was just rented. I know it was only a car, but I felt a kind of stab when she said that – another bit of our old life that was gone forever.

I wondered if Marjorie was looking out as we walked past her driveway. I wondered if she'd seen Mam getting out of the green car.

It's funny to think that Mam and Marjorie used to be pretty friendly, once upon a time.

Anyway, we walked to a little park about ten minutes from the house. Mam seemed a bit quiet on the way, so I told her about Bumble and Catherine Eggleston, and about secondary school, about Henry the pizza delivery boy, and about Ruth Wallace going into hospital for an operation on her legs, and about Dad's disastrous birthday dinner. I didn't talk about the things I really wanted to:

1. The milk attack
2. Chris Thompson
3. How to kiss boys properly.

And I certainly didn't ask the questions I was dying to ask – how long she was staying around, and whether she was thinking about moving back to Ireland. I was afraid to ask, in case the answers weren't the ones I wanted to hear.

When we'd walked about halfway round the park, Mam said, 'Let's sit for a minute,' and when we'd found a bench near some bare-looking trees she took hold of both my hands and told me that she and Dad were going to get a divorce.

And even though it wasn't such a big surprise, even though I'd pretty much stopped hoping that she'd ever come back home, even though I knew deep down that things could never be the same again, it still sounded horrible when she said it. Horrible and empty and – finished. As if a big sign saying 'The End' had suddenly appeared in front of us, like in the old films.

Except that it wasn't a bit like that really, because in the old films people always lived happily ever after.

Luckily, there weren't too many people around to see me crying again, just one old man on another bench who didn't seem to notice, and a couple of little kids who stared at me until their mother called them over.

On the way back from the park, Mam answered the questions I'd been afraid to ask. First she told me she's staying with Granny Daly for three days, which was all the time she could get off work. And then she told me, very gently, that she wasn't planning to move back home for a while yet, but that maybe I could come out and visit her in the summer.

So I had to be happy with that. Funny that the thought of going to America doesn't make me all excited like I thought it would. Maybe when she's back there, it will.

When we got home, she collected her bag from the house, and then she and Dad said goodbye in that same sad, polite way, and I walked back out to the rented car with her.

She hugged me tightly, and whispered that she'd miss me so much, which of course started me crying all over again. I waved until the green car was out of sight, and she hooted the horn as she drove around the corner. I felt so alone, standing there on the path. So empty and alone.

And then I walked back into the house, and I could still smell Mam's almondy smell in the hall, and Dad called out that he was in the sitting room, so I went in because I didn't want to be alone.

We watched some old black-and-white movie on TV that had a lot of hats and singing in it, and we finished off Marjorie's lemon cake, and afterwards Dad gave me €20 to buy myself something nice next time I was in town.

We didn't talk about the divorce. What was there to say?

Seven o'clock, Wednesday, 19th January

Mam flew back to San Francisco today. It's lashing rain outside.

no. 3
DATE

Half past ten, Friday, 21st January.
Tonight I had my third date and my second kiss. This time it was a bit slower, and a bit better (the kiss, I mean). No onions this time, which helped. And no squashed noses.

Can't say it knocked my socks off, though. I mean, it was nice, kind of, but not wildly exciting like it's made out to be on TV and in the movies. Is that all just made up? Is everyone just pretending that kissing is fun? Is it a bit like the emperor's clothes, with everyone thinking it's a bit boring but afraid to say it out loud in case they're wrong?

I wonder if Catherine and Bumble enjoy kissing. She's probably an expert.

I just hope it gets a bit more interesting as we go along.

We got our new French penfriends at school – and guess what? Both Chloe and I got boys, so we don't have to share. That's the good news.

The not-so-good news is that they sent photos, and I have to say that they don't look half as French as I thought they would.

Mine is a bit tubby, and he has really pink podgy cheeks and his ears stick out a bit. Chloe's is slightly better – his eyes are blue, and his hair is dark and cut very short, and he'd probably look quite cool if it wasn't for his nose, which hopefully he'll grow into, and his crooked teeth. Don't they know about braces in France?

My one's name is Joel, which is OK, but Chloe's is called Jean. I know it's the French for John, but when you write it down it just looks girly.

Joel's letter was full of mistakes. Here's one bit:

'My father she owns the library, and my mother rests in the home. Which singers you desire? I desire U2 and the Roling Stones. My anniversary is on December 10 – when is your? I play the rugby after school, he is a cool and funny game, isn't it?'

See what I mean? At the end he wrote, *'Excuse me my badly English'*, which I thought was sweet. I'm sure my French was just as badly when I wrote to him, and I didn't ask to be excused.

OK, I'm going to use the rest of this page for some kissing practice.

Afternoon, Sunday, 6th February.
Mid-term break in a few weeks. And guess what? Dad and I are going to Scotland for five days. And guess what else? Marjorie Maloney is coming with us.

I'm not too sure how I feel about that. I mean, Dad did check with me before he asked her, and I did say OK, but still … it's just that I'm fine with her living across the road from us, and I'm fairly OK about her going out with Dad most weekends, but I don't see why she has to come on holidays with us too.

I know Dad is perfectly free to see whoever he likes, especially now, with the divorce and all, but still, I would REALLY prefer if it stayed just the two of us. We're doing fine. Our cooking is improving, and we hardly ever run out of stuff now. We even buy brown bread sometimes, and I'm cutting down on the coffee. (Still eat far too much Ben & Jerry's though.)

But I have to say that the Scottish trip sounds good.

We're flying into Edinburgh and then getting a train to the little village where we'll be staying. Dad has booked a cottage that he says is over a hundred years old. I can go pony trekking if I want, and we can hire bikes, and there's a restaurant right next door so we can eat out all the time – although I suppose I wouldn't mind if Marjorie felt like cooking dinner once or twice, especially if she does that chocolate dessert thing again.

They just better not share a bedroom, that's all I can say. That would not be OK at *all*.

Right, enough of that. The swimming classes are going great – we've started life-saving, and our coach Sandra says I'm a natural. We'll be giving an exhibition before Easter, using real people instead of dummies. I can't wait for Dad to see me in action.

Maybe someone will get into difficulties when I'm at the beach next summer, and I'll be able to save them.

You're probably wondering how the whole kissing thing is going. Well, we're certainly doing lots of practising, and I suppose it's OK ... I mean, I don't hate it or anything, and Chris is really sweet and funny, and I love his dimple.

And it's nice to have a boyfriend. I know Chloe envies me.

I saw Bumble in town yesterday. He was on his own. He didn't look particularly heartbroken, so I suppose he and Catherine are still together. I almost went over to talk to him, and then I didn't. I don't know why. He was looking in the window of a shoe shop.

I bet Catherine Eggleston doesn't know what kind of shoes he likes.

I still miss him sometimes.

Twenty past six, Monday, 14th February.
I got my very first Valentine's Day card today. I know it's from Chris, although he keeps saying it isn't. He says he doesn't believe in sending cards, that they're just a rip-off, and when we met yesterday he gave me a cute little furry penguin holding a pink heart, which he said was instead of a card.

But I know he sent the card as well.

I mean, it's obvious it's from him. It has a polar bear on the front, saying, 'I can't bear ...' and inside it says, '... being without you,' so it has to be from Chris, doesn't it? A polar bear to go with the penguin.

Of course, if Chris didn't send it, maybe Henry Morrissey did. You know, the gorgeous pizza delivery guy. He knows my address from delivering the pizzas. I wouldn't mind if he'd sent it.

Although I'm pretty sure it's Chris really. But maybe I'll pretend it isn't, just for the heck of it.

A padded envelope arrived from San Francisco today. Inside there was a twenty-dollar note, a three-pack of gorgeous frilly knickers, and a pink furry hat that I wouldn't be seen dead in. Maybe Ruth Wallace would like it. I'll offer it to her next time I see her.

She'll probably tell me to get stuffed.

Her cat's name is Ginger. What a dorky name for a grey cat. I told her I call him Misty, which I think suits him much better, but she said Misty was just the kind of girly name she'd expect me to come up with – which was exactly what I expected *her* to say.

Which kind of made us quits.

She HATES Eminem. She says he's rubbish, but she thinks Colin Farrell is magic. I can't believe we agree on something.

She's had sixteen operations on her legs so far. They think there's a small chance that she'll walk again. When she told me that, she looked a bit fierce, as if she was daring me to laugh.

But I didn't laugh. I was trying to imagine how it must feel like, going into hospital before every operation, thinking 'maybe this time I'll walk out.' Hoping with all your heart sixteen times that you'll never have to sit in that awful wheelchair again, and being disappointed sixteen times.

No wonder she needed someone to be horrible to.

TREKKING

TREKKING
OATCAKES
SCOTLAND'S
EAT!!!!

Half past seven, Monday, 28th February.

We had the best holiday ever in Scotland. It only rained for one day, and the rest of the time it was freezing but dry, and even sunny sometimes, so we bundled up and went pony trekking and cycling, and feeding lambs at the farm of the man who owns the cottages.

I ate haggis – which is a bit like a big round white pudding – and oatcakes, which I wasn't mad about, and homemade fudge that was so delicious I ate far too much and felt sick for about three hours afterwards.

I wanted to try a deep-fried Mars bar, because a girl at school said she had one in Scotland, but we couldn't find them anywhere. Just as well, probably.

My bedroom was tiny. It had a slanted ceiling so low that I could touch every part of it, and a little window just beside my bed. There was a really hairy donkey next door which heehawed at me over a stone wall every morning. I think he thought he was a rooster. I bought a disposable camera in the airport and took loads of photos of everything to show Chloe, including the donkey.

I'm seriously thinking about moving to Scotland when I grow up. I'm not sure about the accent though – it's a bit hard to understand. And they have funny words for things, like 'bairn' for child and 'oatmeal' for porridge (which I didn't have to eat, thank God) and one night Dad drank some whiskey called Sheep Dip, which I would have thought was the worst possible name for any kind of drink.

Nobody said 'hoots mon' at all, which was a bit disappointing. I suppose it's like us saying 'top of the morning'.

I missed Chloe's birthday – it was on while I was away – so I brought her back a wine and green tartan scarf. She's coming over on Saturday and we're going to try baking the lemon cake Marjorie makes. Dad says he's going into hiding, which he thinks is very funny. Poor Dad.

And I have to say that Marjorie was good fun really, not a bit like someone who was practising to be a stepmother. She took no notice of whether I brushed my teeth at bedtime, or how long I spent in the shower, and she didn't worry about my eating enough fruit or fresh vegetables – all the stuff Mam would be thinking about.

Marjorie was more like a big sister, or an aunt, which was just fine by me.

And they didn't share a bedroom. Dad slept on the couch that pulled out into a double bed in the sitting room, and Marjorie and I had the two bedrooms, so everything worked out perfectly in the end. Funny how you can worry about something that turns out to be nothing. I'm never going to worry again about things that haven't happened, only about things that have.

Which means that I'm not going to worry about whether I get to San Francisco in the summer or not. I'm not going to worry that Mam hasn't mentioned it since she got back.

After all, summer is still a long, long way away.

By the way, Chris is in another show at school. This time they're doing Camelot, and he's the knight Lancelot, who I always preferred to King Arthur. He says Bumble is playing a knight too, and he even has some lines on his own, which is nice.

It'll be on just before Easter. Chloe and I will go to see them, of course. And maybe Ruth would like to come with us – I'll ask her.

Wonder if Bumble's still going out with Catherine. I suppose she'll be in the show too. She's probably planning to be a movie star when she leaves school. She certainly has the brains for it, ha ha.

Half eight, Friday, first week of March

I can't believe that a whole year has gone by since I began to write in this diary. I've just read the first entry again, and it made me laugh – I'd completely forgotten about throwing that bowl of porridge at Dad. What a kid I was then.

Not that we don't still have rows every now and again. Last weekend he got mad at me for coming in after ten o'clock, when every other thirteen-year-old I know in the world is allowed out till at least half past ten on a Saturday night.

But the nice thing about Dad is that he never stays mad at you for long, not like some people who sulk for days. Chris Thompson has been sulking for four and a half days exactly.

Just because I happened to mention the gorgeous pizza guy to a few girls. Just as a joke – of course I wasn't serious. Any normal person could see I was joking. But Chris was not amused. He asked me how I'd like it if *he* went around swooning over other girls – as if I was swooning over Henry. Some people are so childish.

And he keeps going on about that Valentine card, keeps saying I must know who sent it. I'm beginning to think that maybe he really didn't send it after all. Maybe it really *was* Henry, although I've met him a few times since then and he doesn't seem any different. He's friendly and chatty, but he's always been like that.

Bet *he* wouldn't get all sulky, if I was kidding around with my friends.

Well, if Chris Thompson thinks I'm going to pick up the phone and apologise, he's got another think coming.

I got another letter from France. Joel is obviously keen to learn English, and I must say he has a lot to learn. Here's a bit of his last letter:

'He is raining in Paris now. All the days raining, no sunshine. How is Irish climate? My papa is went in Toulouse in south of France for bussines, he must bargain with the books. The last days I had playing rugby with my freinds. Do you enjoy to play sport?'

Chloe isn't having much better luck with Jean. He asked her if she was '*going in cinema many*'. We haven't a clue what he meant.

EXHIBIT TIME

Twenty-five past seven, Thursday, 17th March.
We had our life-saving exhibition last night. Dad came, of course, and Chloe and her parents. Everyone else had a few people there too, so the place was quite crowded, and I was kind of nervous before my turn, but it went fine, thank goodness.

(Of course I wished Mam was there, but I'm getting used to her missing stuff. Still no mention of my going to San Francisco. She's probably planning to surprise me with the plane ticket, so I won't say anything.)

Afterwards, Sandra gave a little speech, and then we were each presented with certificates and selection boxes, and while we got changed everyone had sandwiches and drinks in the lobby. I had to practically drag Dad away, which wasn't a bit like him – usually he can't wait to get away from groups of people like that. But I suppose he doesn't get out much, except with Marjorie.

Although, now that I come to think of it, he hasn't met Marjorie for a while. I wonder if they've had a row.

By the way, I met Damien Wallace, Ruth's brother, just a while ago. I called over with a pack of Maltesers that I didn't want from the selection box. Maltesers annoy me, the way they stick in your teeth and then melt away into nothing. But I remembered there was a box of them on Ruth's locker in the hospital, so I thought she may as well have them.

Damien answered the door and told me that Ruth was gone shopping with their mother. I gave him the Maltesers and he promised to give them to her, and then he said, 'I like your top – the colour suits you.'

It was so unexpected that I could think of nothing to say, so I just smiled and turned away.

It's just an old green top, that I put on just for the laugh since it's St Patrick's Day. But it was nice of him to say that. Maybe I should wear green more often.

Funny, I never noticed before, but Damien Wallace has got the longest eyelashes.

Oh by the way, Chris and I have made up. He phoned me in the end, and I told him I didn't mean to make him cross when I joked about Henry. It wasn't exactly an apology, more a kind of meeting in the middle. I suppose that's how it goes with boyfriends. Chris is pretty busy these days, rehearsing for the Camelot show, but we're going out for a pizza tomorrow night with Terry McNamara (remember Catherine Eggleston's ex?) and his new girlfriend. Must remember to make sure Chris doesn't order onions.

Half past eight, Tuesday, 29th March.

I'm in mourning. I want to cry.

Today I saw Henry, the pizza guy, in town with his arm around a girl. She was at least seventeen, maybe older, and she looked like a model. Her legs were about a mile long, and she had really shiny, jet-black hair, and her make-up was perfect.

She had her hand in the back pocket of Henry's jeans, which I think looks dead cheap, but Henry didn't seem to mind. He smiled when he saw me and said, 'Hey, doll,' and the girl gave me a filthy look, and I felt like a kid in my old jeans and my vomit-coloured jacket. And wouldn't you know, I hadn't even bothered to put lipstick on.

Well, I *was* only meeting Chloe.

So Henry's got a girlfriend. I suppose I shouldn't be surprised. It would be more surprising if he didn't – he's so good-looking and friendly. And imagine I thought he liked me, just because he chatted a bit when he brought our pizzas, and winked at me when he was leaving.

And remember I thought the Valentine card I got might be from him? Boy, I must have a really good imagination. I just hope he didn't guess how I felt about him.

Oh well, at least I still have Chris.

Ruth came over here yesterday after dinner and we played Monopoly with Dad. She's a really sneaky player, like I knew she would be. She cheated all the time, snuck out of jail and robbed money from the bank and changed the dice when she thought we weren't looking.

Dad said it was a good job she was in a wheelchair, or he'd have asked her to step outside, and she told him she'd report him to Childline, if he laid a finger on her. They got on really well.

I was glad to see Dad enjoying himself. I think I was right about him and Marjorie having a row – they haven't gone out for ages. And I haven't seen any sign of her around the neighbourhood, although her car's still there. Maybe she's avoiding us. Hopefully they'll make up soon. Dad needs someone to go out with now and again.

I can't believe I just wrote that – remember how mad I was when Dad told me he was going out with Marjorie the first time? Funny how things change, isn't it?

Or maybe I'm just getting more sensible in my old age, ha ha.

Ruth is coming with Chloe and me to the *Camelot*

show at the Comp on Saturday night. Wonder what she'll think of Chris.

Wonder if Bumble and Catherine are still going out. I could ask Chris but I'd better not, in case he gets the wrong idea. Remember how touchy he was about Henry? And he knows how friendly I used to be with Bumble.

Henry with a girlfriend, Bumble deserting me, Chris sulking about nothing. Really, I'm beginning to wonder if boys are worth all the trouble they cause.

my coach! weird!! my DAD?

OK, this is weird.

Dad has just gone out to meet Sandra. In case you've forgotten, she's my swimming coach.

Remember the life-saving exhibition, a couple of weeks ago? Remember I had to nearly drag Dad home that night? I should have suspected something then – I mean, Dad would usually be the first to leave something like that. He's never been what you might call a good mixer – Mam was much better at that kind of stuff.

I remember Dad moaning whenever he and Mam would go out to meet other couples. He'd warn Mam not to leave him on his own, he'd keep saying that he was no good at 'making small talk', which I think means discussing boring stuff like the weather and the government, and things like that.

I'm trying to remember if he talked much to Sandra

on the night of the exhibition, but I just didn't notice. I suppose he must have spent some time with her though – enough to get her phone number anyway, or ask her if she had a boyfriend, or something.

Anyway, I'd completely forgotten about that night. So when Dad told me earlier that he and Sandra were going to a play, it was a real surprise.

Does this mean that it's all finished with Marjorie then? I wonder if I'll ever find out what happened there. I thought they were fine in Scotland, but as far as I can tell they haven't met since.

And now something just feels weird. I mean, I'm the teenager in this house. I'm the one supposed to be going out on dates and stuff, right? Dad is supposed to be the one sitting at home waiting for me to come back, watching the clock to make sure I'm on time. But I'm staying in tonight – Chris went to Dublin for the weekend – and Dad is out on the town.

It just seems a bit the wrong way around, that's all.

Sandra is nice. She's quite pretty and fairly slim, and a great swimmer – not that that matters, of course, unless you're drowning and she's nearby. She's about Dad's age, I'd say, or maybe a bit younger. And I suppose she's single, and there's nothing wrong with the idea of her going out with a soon-to-be-divorced man.

But I'm kind of sorry about Marjorie, just when I was getting to like her too. It's all a bit confusing, and I'm not sure how I feel about it really.

I think I'll go next door and see what Ruth thinks. Not that she'd have much of a clue, with her parents still together and probably madly in love and everything, but it would be good just to talk to someone, and Ruth usually has something interesting to say.

Insulting, but interesting.

You know what Ruth thinks? That Dad and Marjorie have had a row, and that he's trying to make her jealous now with Sandra. And you know, she could be right. Aren't grown-ups funny, the games they play?

Ruth's brother Damien was there when I went over, watching TV in the living room. He came into the kitchen to make popcorn while Ruth and I were talking, and he put some in a bowl for us, which was nice of him.

When he'd gone back to the sitting room, I asked Ruth if he had a girlfriend, just out of curiosity, and she gave me kind of a funny look and said no. Maybe he's gay, which would be a shame.

For other girls, I mean. Not for me, because I've got Chris.

And anyway, Damien Wallace isn't interested in me in the slightest. I'm probably just a kid to him.

Ginger the cat followed me home, and while I was feeding him some cheese that had gone a bit mouldy, I got a brilliant idea. I'll ask Dad if I can get a kitten for my birthday, which is just a couple of weeks away. There's a Cats' Home about half an hour's drive from here, and they're bound to have loads.

I'd like a white one with orange markings. I'll probably call her Molly (of course she'll be a girl) and she'll sleep at the bottom of my bed, and play with Ginger by day when I'm at school.

The only pet I ever had was a goldfish, when I was about six. I called him Flipper, and Bumble and I used to bring his bowl out the back so he could watch us playing. I remember once we forgot to bring him back in, and Dad was reading me a story in bed when I remembered. Poor Flipper died about a week later. Dad said it had nothing to do with leaving him outside, but I still felt guilty for ages.

Maybe I could get two kittens, Molly and Polly.

The *Camelot* show is on tomorrow night at the Comp. Ruth is coming. Her Dad is going to drive us there, and we'll meet Chloe in the lobby. I'm dying to see what Ruth thinks of Chris – I've told her about him, but she hasn't met him yet.

Oh by the way, she loved the furry pink hat Mam sent me, and it actually looks quite good on her. So as Granny Daly would say, *FOR EVERY OLD FOOT THERE'S AN OLD BOOT.*

Very late, Saturday, 2nd April.

I've just got home from the show. Are you ready for the big news?

Bumble and Catherine have broken up.

And *he* broke up with *her*, not the other way around.

And guess what else? He told Liam O'Callaghan that it's because he fancies another girl.

Can you believe it?

Trudy Higgins told us, at the interval. She said Catherine was really upset. She said Catherine fancied Bumble for ages in primary school – which would explain why she was always so unfriendly to me. Trudy said the only reason Catherine went out with Terry McNamara was to make Bumble jealous.

I repeat, can you believe it?

I could hardly concentrate on the second half of the show, my head was spinning so much. I was so sure that Bumble would be the one who ended up broken-hearted.

I tried to feel sorry for Catherine, really I did. But somehow I kept remembering the bitchy comments she'd make about me at school, and how she'd only been using poor Terry all the time to try and make Bumble jealous, and it was very hard to have sympathy for her.

She was in the show too, but she only had a small part this time – one of Queen Guinevere's ladies-in-waiting – and she and Bumble were never onstage together, which was probably just as well. Chris was a pretty good Sir Lancelot, and a girl I didn't know was brilliant as Guinevere.

Dad was coming to drive Chloe, Ruth and me home after the show, but I told him I'd ring him when we were ready, because I wanted Ruth to meet Chris. So we were hanging around near the dressing rooms afterwards when who should come out but Bumble.

I hadn't spoken to him since the night of my first date with Chris – just a few months ago, but it seemed longer. He said hello to Chloe and me, and I introduced him to Ruth, and he tried not to look surprised that we were together (remember he was the only one who knew about how nasty Ruth had been to me?).

We chatted for a bit, and then Bumble said he and I must meet up for a Coke some time to catch up, and I said that'd be nice, and then Chris came out, and while I was introducing him to Ruth, Bumble did a disappearing act.

I don't think we'll be meeting up. It's just something people say, isn't it?

On the way home, Ruth said she thought Chris was

nice. She must have been too tired to think up something rude.

I haven't mentioned that Chris is my boyfriend to Dad yet. There's no rush.

freedom.

Ten to six, Friday 15th April – Easter holidays.
Hurrah – two weeks of freedom from school. And my birthday is next week – the day before Easter Sunday, actually. Can't believe I'm going to be fourteen. I haven't decided what I want to do for it yet. Dad will probably suggest going out to dinner, because we did that last year, but maybe I'll do something with Chris instead.

Or maybe with Chloe and Ruth.

The thing is, I'm not all that sure how I feel about Chris right now.

I mean, I hardly ever think about him when we're apart, and I don't really get excited at the thought of seeing him. We're going out tonight, and I couldn't care less. And I'm pretty sure it wouldn't break my heart if we were finished. I tried imagining not going out with him any more, and it didn't make me sad at all.

And I have to say the whole kissing thing hasn't got

any better, even though we practise all the time. It's just – well, sort of boring really.

Maybe I'll ask Ruth what she thinks. I know she hasn't had any experience with boys, but she's pretty clever. She might have some advice about what I should do.

Actually, I kind of know what I should do myself, but I think I just want to hear someone else telling me.

Dad said some boy rang for me yesterday when I was next door at Ruth's. He says it sounded like Bumble, but I'm pretty sure it was Chris. I might ring him back later.

It definitely looks like Dad and Marjorie are finished. I saw her a few days ago, working in her garden, and she waved across, but I didn't think she looked as cheery as normal. I wonder if it's awkward for her now, living right across the road from Dad. Poor Marjorie.

I don't know how Dad's date with my swimming coach Sandra went last week, because I was in bed by the time he got home, and he didn't mention it the next day. I don't know about you, but I can NOT talk to my father about his dates – it just feels too weird. So I'll have to wait and see what happens there.

By the way, I asked Dad about getting a kitten for my birthday, and he said, 'We'll see.' I don't think he's much of a cat lover really. He usually ignores Ginger if he sees him in our garden. I'll just have to do a bit of nagging; I'm good at that. Dad says if nagging was an Olympic sport I'd win gold.

I've told him the colour kitten I'd like, and I reminded him that the Cats' Home is always looking for good owners, and he just grunted, but that could have been because his mouth was full of fish fingers at the time.

I told Ruth I was hoping to get a kitten, and she said I was such a copycat, and I told her that I wasn't, because a cute little kitten beats a mangy old cat any day. But I tickled Ginger under his chin while I was saying it, so he'd know I was only joking.

Joel wrote again from France. Here's a bit of his latest letter:

'I and my papa go to skiing next week. I enjoy to ski very much, but the last times I had broke my ankle-bone, and she was very much painfull. Did you went to ski in Ireland?'

Good God. I wonder if my French sounds as bad to him. Maybe Marjorie would help me out with my next letter. It might cheer her up a bit. I could call over tomorrow and ask her.

Joel wants me to send a photo, so just for fun I'm going to cut Catherine Eggleston's picture out of the yearbook we got at the end of sixth class, and send him that. Chloe doesn't approve, but I don't care. Joel will never know it's not me, and he might as well think he has a beautiful penfriend.

I don't take in the pizzas from Henry any more. I let Dad answer the door now. I'm still mourning a bit, but I'm not that heartbroken really. I suppose it was just a crush, and not true love.

Wonder how you know when it's true love? Must ask Ruth.

Mam still hasn't mentioned anything about me going out to see her in the summer. I refuse to worry.

JUST A CRUSH

not true love.

Afternoon, Saturday, 16th April.

Ruth Wallace is the most annoying person I ever lived next door to.

Remember I said I was going to talk to her about Chris? Well, I did, and she said exactly what I thought she would – that clearly I wasn't interested, and that I should finish with him. I had to agree, since I'd already figured that out for myself.

Then we decided that I had to meet him face to face, that it wasn't nice to do something like that over the phone. Ruth told me I had to say that it wasn't him, it was me. She says that's the kind way of breaking up with someone.

I don't know how Ruth knows stuff like that, but she does.

Anyway, when we had all that sorted out, and I was getting up to go home, Ruth said, 'I know something you don't.' And she had this really smug look on her face.

So of course I said, 'What are you talking about?'

And she said, 'I can't say any more.'

Is there anything more annoying than someone telling you they know something you don't, and then not telling you what it is?

Then I said I'd push her out of the wheelchair, if she didn't tell me, which of course didn't scare her a bit. But she did take pity on me, because she said, 'Look, I really can't tell you who it is – I'd be killed – but I know someone who fancies you.'

And no matter how much I threatened her after that – I even went to her fridge and took out an almost-full litre of milk – she wouldn't say another word.

Of course she could be making it all up – but why? We're friends now. She doesn't try and wind me up any more. Well, she does – last week she asked me if I ever thought of getting my head shaved and wearing a wig – but it's only a bit of fun now, and I just tell her to get stuffed.

But this is different, and I don't think she's making it up. I just can't imagine who it could be though. The only boys we both know are Chris and Bumble – unless it's someone Ruth knows and I don't. But how could someone I don't even know fancy me? It doesn't make sense.

It's kind of nice though, to think that someone thinks you're cool.

I'm still working on the birthday kitten idea with Dad. He won't give me a definite yes, but that's probably because he's going to surprise me. I can read him like a book sometimes.

I really hope he gets a mostly white one, although of course I'll take any kitten he gives me. As Granny Daly would say, *BEGGARS CAN'T BE CHOOSERS.*

Oh and guess what? Dad was right – it *was* Bumble who phoned the other night. He rang again last evening, and would you believe he actually meant it about us meeting up after all? We settled on next Thursday – I kind of want to get the whole breaking up with Chris thing over with first.

I am NOT looking forward to that. Better ring Chris now and arrange to meet him in town. God, I hope he hasn't got me a birthday present yet – hope he didn't pick up on the hints I was dropping about White Musk.

NOT YOU! awful. awful. just awful

NOT YOU! awful.awful. just awful

Evening, Monday, 18th April.

Well, I did it. It was awful, just awful.

I met him at our usual corner, and we went to Nosh and ordered Cokes, and he started telling me about his little sister's birthday party the day before, and right in the middle of the bit when his sister's best friend got sick into the bowl of trifle, I butted in, because I couldn't bear it any longer, and I said, 'Chris, I have something to say.'

And he just sat there, while I stuttered and stammered and told him it was me, not him, and how sorry I was, and his face went red and his eyes filled with tears, and I felt like a total monster.

And when I ran out of words, we just sat there for a bit, and I kept my eyes on the paper tablecloth, where Chris had been doodling stars while he was telling me about the birthday party. Then he kind of pulled himself together and stood up and said he had to go.

I could see he was really struggling not to cry in front of me, so I just nodded and let him walk out, and I stayed sitting there for about twenty minutes, to give him plenty of time to get away.

Breaking up sure stinks. I hope I never have to do it again. I think I'd rather if someone broke up with me, even if it made me really sad. It couldn't be worse than feeling the way I do now.

Anyway, I wanted to talk to someone after that, so I called into Ruth on the way home, and she told me that I'd done the right thing, and that of course I wasn't a monster, which was just what I needed to hear.

Imagine I thought she was horrible once. Just shows how wrong you can be.

She still refuses to tell me who fancies me – not that I want to get involved with anyone else right now. I think I've had enough of boys for a while.

Wouldn't mind knowing who it was though.

Very early in the morning, Saturday, 23rd April.
Happy Birthday to me.

Hurrah that it's a Saturday, so there's no school. There's also no sign of a kitten – I've just been downstairs to check – so Dad must be planning to take me to the Cats' Home later to let me choose one for myself, which I was secretly hoping he'd do. He's still in bed, which isn't surprising, considering it's only half past six in the morning.

So while I'm waiting for him to get up, I may as well tell you about meeting Bumble on Thursday.

You know what? It was as if we'd never been apart.

Of course he was late, like he always was, and I tried to look cross when he walked in, like I always used to do, and he managed to smile and look guilty at the same time, and I hadn't the heart to give out to him.

Just like it always was.

I don't know who talked more, him or me. I know we

ordered two lots of Coke, and then we got chips, because suddenly it was lunchtime. He told me I looked more grown-up, which is a good thing to hear when you're almost fourteen, and I told him he needed a haircut, which he did.

And somewhere in between the first and second Coke, Bumble started talking about Catherine Eggleston.

He told me that going out with her had been a big mistake – that he'd never been interested in her, not really. He said he just laughed when Trudy Higgins told him that Catherine fancied him. He really didn't believe her, until Catherine herself asked him out, less than a week after she finished with Terry McNamara. *She* asked *him* out – imagine.

And because she was beautiful, and because it was nice to think that someone like her was interested in him, Bumble said yes. I suppose most boys would say yes to Catherine Eggleston.

And for a while he enjoyed being with her. He liked seeing other boys looking at her when they were out together, and she could even be quite good fun sometimes. But in the end, it wasn't enough – he just wasn't interested, so he finished with her.

And then I told him about Chris, and how awful it had been finishing with him, and we agreed that breaking up really sucked.

It was just lovely to be with Bumble again. I told him all about Ruth, and about Mam turning up out of the blue after Christmas. He and Mam always got on – I think Mam secretly thought of Bumble as my future husband. You know what mams are like.

Anyway, just before we said goodbye he gave me a little padded envelope and told me not to open it until my birthday, and it's here in front of me now, and I think it's about time I found out what's in it.

A quarter past seven

It's a bottle of White Musk, with a card that says, 'Just make sure you don't wear it when you're meeting me.' He's so romantic.

Right, I can't bear the kitten suspense any longer. Time to go downstairs and make lots of noise in the kitchen.

A quarter to eight

OK, I've had three sausages and two rashers, and there's still no sign of Dad. Is he ever getting up?

Hang on, someone's at the front door.

Nine o'clock

Molly is the cutest kitten you ever saw.

She's like a ball of fur, white with orange paws and ears, and she's got the tiniest little mew, and her tongue feels like the dark grey end of a rubber, the end that rubs out ink, and her tail is short and fat and fluffy, and the little pink pads under her paws are just adorable.

She's already eaten half a tin of sardines and two saucers of kitten milk, and she's got a milk moustache. She sneezed a minute ago, and she nearly fell over.

I want to eat her up, she's so gorgeous.

You know where I found her? Sitting on the doormat in a Tayto box with a red ribbon around it and holes punched in the sides. Dad sneaked downstairs with her when I was having breakfast and put her on the mat and rang the bell and hid around the corner until I came out and found her.

He kept her in his room last night.

Did you get that? My Dad, who really doesn't like cats, spent the whole night with a mewing little kitten in his room, just so she'd be a surprise for me on my birthday. Is he the best dad in the world or what?

Hang on, the post has just come, and there's an envelope from Mam. Hopefully containing a few dollars.

Ten past nine

You won't believe it. It's a return ticket to San Francisco. I'm flying out on the tenth of July and coming back on the sixth of August.

Almost a whole month with her. I'm so happy I could cry.

Ten to seven in the evening

Ruth loves Molly. She didn't say one insulting thing about her, not that I'd care. Not after she gave me a year's subscription to Mizz, which she said I was getting on condition that I passed them all on to her. I told her I'd think about it.

Chloe loves Molly too. She gave me *The Monster Cookie Book* for my birthday. It's the size of an encyclopaedia, and it must have about two hundred cookie recipes in it.

She and Ruth almost fought over who'd hold Molly and naturally Ruth won. They're both gone home now, and I'm just about to start getting ready to go out to dinner with Dad. I decided that's what I wanted to do most of all this evening.

Hang on – the doorbell's just rung, and Dad's in the shower, so I'd better answer it.

Half past seven

Dad has just knocked on my door and said if we don't get moving, they'll give our table away. I told him I'd be out in a sec.

You'll never guess who was at the front door.

He was holding out a little bag, and he looked a bit shy. He said, 'I just wanted to wish you happy birthday.'

I took the bag and opened it, and inside was a little sparkly red collar that looked as if it would fit perfectly around Molly's neck. And when I looked back up at him, something happened.

My stomach flipped, in a really nice kind of way.

And suddenly I felt shy myself, and all I could do was smile and say, 'Thank you, it's lovely.'

And then he said, 'Maybe we could go out some time.'

And I said, 'I'd like that.' And I watched him turn around and walk back next door.

I wonder what it'll be like, kissing Damien Wallace.

As Granny Daly would say, *YOU JUST NEVER KNOW WHAT'S WAITING AROUND THE CORNER.*

We hope you enjoyed meeting Liz.
Now meet Tia and Tammy in *Blue Lavender Girl*
and *Copper Girl* from Judy May.

From *Blue Lavender Girl* by Judy May

I'm glad I didn't waste brain cells thinking of anything else to do for the summer, because I just found out that I'm going to Aunt Maisie's anyway. She always comes here so I've never seen her place. Mum tells me it's a large cottage in its own grounds, but if she thinks that will change me into one of those *Pride and Prejudice* girls she's very much mistaken.

I'm sort of relieved though, because I hate everyone right now, but I won't let them know that.

I need to use every minute I have to make it so they won't go into my room while I'm away. That way they can't pull another stunt like the salmon-coloured flowered wallpaper that appeared when I was off on the weekend school trip to that farm. I am going to push all the mess near the door so it's impossible to get through.

I put all my favourite clothes into a big suitcase and then took them all out again deciding to wash everything first in case she doesn't have a washing machine. I know she will, I just ... God, I don't know.

I went around to meet Kira and Dee at the burger place, but they sounded worse than my mother. They kept saying that I'd have a good time and they wish they were going and that I might find a boyfriend there.

I didn't even get to say goodbye properly because Dee's brother's friends arrived in, and this needed the girls' full attention.

***

I looked up at the sky and wondered what's happened to the stars these days. There are never any when I think to look up. When I was really little and we spent time in Dad's uncle's place by the beach, there were loads of stars. We used to all lie on the beach and Dad would teach us the names of the stars and Mum would get them all muddled up and not on purpose. It was such a laugh, but I haven't explained it very well. It was one of those 'you-had-to-have-been-there' things.

I nearly forgot to pack this diary, good thing it was on top of my jeans with the beads otherwise I would have left it behind. It's weird that I have written more in this than in English class for the last year.

***

I am in bed early.

PRETEND REASON: To get enough sleep to be up bright and early to get to the train in time.

REAL REASON: I am so angry with my parents that I keep wanting to bite someone's head off whenever either of them says anything, and I don't want to fall out with them just before I go or they might never let me come home.

From *Copper Girl* by Judy May

        10 June (end of first week of holidays)
Another day minding Mikey and restocking shelves in the
shop. Thrillsville. Now that I have a diary I have to do
something big or my head will fall off. I solemnly swear that
by the end of the summer I will have:

  1. Met a rock star or a film star and had a proper
conversation with them.
  2. Started going out with one of the Rat Pack guys,
preferably Johnny Saunders.
  3. Got myself on television doing something non-
embarrassing.
  4. ANYTHING that no one I know has ever done, just to
stick it to Adie O'Boyle and her lot.

Once I do that Johnny will really notice me and I'll finally get to go out with him, or even maybe one of the other Rat Pack guys if I decide I'm too big for him. The look on Johnny's face if he asked me out and I turned him down, that would be priceless! Then I will send Hellie and Charlie a really casual e-mail and tell them all about it like as if it's nothing. Yeah, I wish.

Pete laughs at the Rat Pack guys (Hellie came up with the name from some old musicians her Dad likes) – he calls them snobs and says they aren't worthy to lick his boots, so I remind him he only ever wears sneakers. I think he's just jealous of Johnny and his friends because they are all from rich families and are impossibly good-looking and go to a better school than him. It's a pity because if he was friends with them I'd find it easier to get to know them and wouldn't only say three sentences to Johnny on the odd Friday night at the Club. I was thinking of telling Pete about how much I want to go out with Johnny, but I know he'd just make my life hell about it. Sometimes he acts like my big brother, which is mostly OK.

Right, I am now going to dress in something cool and get into town before 3pm and make something happen. I will get inspired and make a plan or maybe even meet someone and have a life-changing conversation.

LATER

I didn't get into town until five because Mum made me tidy my room first. So it's entirely her fault that all the interesting people on the planet had gone home by then.

Other books in the Journals series from The O'Brien Press

Blue Lavender Girl by Judy May
ISBN 0-86278-991-5
978-0-86278-991-6

Copper Girl by Judy May
ISBN 0-86278-990-7
978-0-86278-990-9